The Acting Bug

For Yan, of course

© 1995 Kathryn Ellis

Boardwalk Books

Canadian Catalogue in Publication Data

Ellis, Kathryn, 1955–
    The acting bug

(Backbeat)
ISBN 1–895681–10–3

I. Title.   II. Series

PS8559.L558A73 1995   jC813'.54   C95–931666–3
PZ7.E55Ac 1995

Design, Electronic Composition, and Production by
Blair Kerrigan/Glyphics

Cover Illustration by June Lawrason

BACKBEAT

The Acting Bug

Kathryn Ellis

Boardwalk Books

One

"I can't believe it's only the second day of summer vacation — I'm already B-O-R-E-D!" moaned Kate Merriman to her best friend, Maria Lococco. She grabbed her sandy blonde curls and pulled at them in frustration.

"Oh, come on, Kate, don't be so dramatic," laughed Maria. "We've got art classes to look forward to . . . we can go swimming . . . "

Kate cut her off. "We went swimming yesterday. I look hideous in a bathing suit. At least you've got a figure . . . and I hate you for your dark skin. Italians! I look like an unbaked breadstick in mine."

Maria laughed again. "You do not!"

"It's not the point, anyway. I want to *do* something. Fun! Excitement!"

"Do you want to go downtown?" asked Maria. "Go shopping? See a movie?"

"Do you think our parents would let us?"

Though Kate was almost thirteen, and Maria had already turned, their parents were only starting to allow them to go out on their own, and downtown was . . . well, downtown. But still . . .

"Sure," Maria replied. "You just have to work them right. If we make all the plans and show them we're responsible, they can't say no."

"I don't know . . . " said Kate. "My dad . . . "

By now Maria had grabbed the newspaper from the coffee table in Kate's basement rec room where the girls were sitting to escape from the summer heat. "What movie do you want to see?"

"What movie is there that we can get into?" asked Kate. "I wish we were fourteen."

"We could pass."

"Forget it. We might be able to get in, but what would we tell our parents? If we lied, they'd never let us go out again."

"You're right," sighed Maria. "Well, there must be *some*thing we can go to." She began flipping the pages of the entertainment section.

"Just not something too sucky, and nothing with slobbery dogs. They totally gross me out," said Kate.

But Maria had stopped listening. "Listen to this," she said. " 'Young actors wanted for new television series. The producers of the critically acclaimed children's program *Roller Skates* are embarking on a new project called *Backbeat*. Actors aged ten to fifteen years, with or without experience, should call 555–3452 for applications.' We should try out, Kate! Who knows, it could be a laugh!"

"It's probably a scam. You probably have to pay for it," said Kate. But it did sound like fun.

"It's not an ad, it's in the real part of the paper," Maria pointed out. "Let's at *least* find out. It'd be like *Peter Pan* — only better." Kate and Maria had first come to know each other in grade six in the school production of the play. They had both been pirates, and in the scene where they capture the Lost Boys, the girls had to kidnap a very annoying grade four kid who was always sniffing, and never had a Kleenex, and seemed intent on stepping on their feet as many times as he could.

But Kate wasn't reminiscing about *Peter Pan*. "Come on, Maria. Why would they make a television show in an ordinary city like Lakeview? They do that stuff in Hollywood or New York — or somewhere else."

"Maybe they think Lakeview looks like every other city on the planet — which it does."

"I guess," said Kate who, in spite of her doubts, was getting into the spirit. "Or maybe they're not *making* the show here, just auditioning here because Lakeview–ites look like the 'ites' of every other city on the planet."

"Anyway," Maria went on, "they *are* doing it — it says so in the paper. I'm going to call for an application. Come on!" Maria was already halfway up the stairs to the phone in Kate's kitchen.

Kate could hardly believe they were actually going through with this. A minute ago she hadn't been sure she'd be allowed to go and *see* a film, and now she was thinking of being *in* one — or in a TV show, anyway. But Maria always had such great schemes, and unlike Kate's crazy ideas they actually worked out a lot of the time. Anyhow, there was no stopping Maria once she got started on something, and she was already dialling the number from the newspaper. And Kate was getting infected with Maria's energy.

"Yes, let's do it," she said. "It'll be great! They'll whisk us all off to wear sunglasses in Hollywood and go surfing! Maybe we'll get on TV — be big stars, get our own dressing rooms, drive around in limos. We'd never, *ever* be bored!'

• • •

In the end, it had taken a lot of diplomacy, a little begging, and her mom's help for Kate's father to even consider letting her apply for the television show. Kate's mom was okay about it from the start, but her dad gruffly echoed Kate's first suspicions that it was a scam — or worse. Then, he got worried that Kate might be upset if she didn't pass the audition. Next, it was her mom worrying about what would happen if she did get a part and missed too much school. Kate promised to keep her marks up and finally got her mom to side with her.

"Honey," her mom pleaded, "just let her try. She might have fun."

"Fun?" her dad snapped. "How do we know this is even on the level?"

Kate knew it was time to be as invisible as possible, as she pushed mashed potatoes around her plate and let her mother win the argument for her. Maybe it was because her dad was a lawyer that he suspected everyone and everything, but he never seemed to trust Kate out of the house. Her parents were so different that way. It was like her mother trusted the world and her father didn't. It always went this way whenever something new came up. Kate knew her dad was just looking out for her, but sometimes she wished he wouldn't look out so *hard*.

"We'll check it out," her mom was saying, "I'll call tomorrow. I think it would be good for Kate to get out of the house more." There was a dangerous tone to her mother's voice.

The last thing Kate wanted was for an argument to start.

"It's okay," said Kate. "I don't really have to . . . "

But her dad interrupted her. "No, go ahead. Have some fun." Abruptly he left the room, taking his wine glass with him. Kate sighed. Moments later, as she knew would happen, the soothing, lush sounds of Beethoven's *Moonlight Sonata* drifted down the stairs.

"It's okay, honey," said Kate's mom. "I think your dad's just having a bad day. We'll check it out, but you apply for this TV thing. It'll be good experience, even if you don't get a part. You'll still be our smart, beautiful Kate."

Kate smiled at her mother, but she went to bed a little upset that night. She knew that it wasn't just a bad day, that her dad was apt to react quickly to new things, but that he usually got used to the idea, whatever it was, in the end. But Kate was beginning to get tired of having to duck every time something happened, in case her dad went off the deep end over it. It was bad enough when it was just the three of them, but she hated it when it happened with other people around. She hated going to restaurants with her family, because no matter what her dad ordered, it seemed the restaurant would always be

6

"just out." He wouldn't yell at the waitress or anything, but you could tell he was annoyed, and it embarrassed Kate. Worse was having friends from school over, since she could never predict what kind of mood he would be in — sometimes Kate thought that just having strangers in the house unexpectedly was what annoyed him, though he was always polite, of course. Except Maria. Kate knew she could have Maria over anytime. She knew about Kate's dad, and she understood. Things were always okay with Maria.

• • •

In the end, Kate's application was sent in with a parent's signature and snapshot. So was Maria's — and here they were, sitting in the reception area of Rolling Films, waiting to be auditioned.

Along with about a million other kids, way more gorgeous than either of them. Kate knew she didn't stand a chance. Some of the kids even seemed to know each other; some had been models in catalogues or had been in commercials before. They all sat on the plushy gray chairs that lined the reception room, reading over sheets of paper they had been given that the lady had called "sides." They were like little parts out of a play, with lines for only one person. The lady said they didn't have to memorize the lines, but they might like to look them over.

Kate had looked them over, and now she was taking in the room. It was fairly large, and on one wall was a glass case full of plaques and trophies and certificates and medals. Kate couldn't believe this company had won so many awards, that there were so many awards to win. She even recognized one trophy — an Emmy. She remembered having seen it on TV, a lady with wings holding a hollow ball in the air. The wings were so long and pointed, Kate thought, you could almost use them for letter openers. She could imagine the statuette sitting on someone's desk — maybe the one belonging to the lady who had given them the "sides." She pictured her efficiently opening two letters at a time on the wings, and giggled nervously at the image.

"What?" asked Maria, looking up from her paper.

"Nothing," said Kate. She didn't think it would look too good for her to be laughing at the company's awards. She would tell Maria later, when they could have a laugh over it. Everything in the room made her feel like a total loser. The Emmy. All the other awards. The lady who had given them their sides with her ultra-fashionable glasses and severe black outfit. The expensive gray chairs. The other kids. Especially the other kids. The tanned girl with the silky blonde hair. The next tanned girl with the silky blonde hair. *Another* tanned girl with silky blonde hair. The redhead with big turquoise eyes. The elegant Asian girl whose hair was so long she could sit on it. The dramatic-looking black girl with the huge wooden earrings. That really, really cute guy with dark hair that fell into his eyes and a nice, friendly, crooked smile.

Maria might get in — maybe. Maria had a figure and a pretty face and nice black hair. Maria had even had a line in *Peter Pan* : "To the ship!" But not Kate. Kate with her gawky elbows, her glasses, her slightly weird clothing combinations, her nondescript hair — neither dark nor fair, neither long nor short, curlyish but never in the right places. Not Kate.

Suddenly it was her turn. Her name was called. She thought she heard Maria whisper, "Good luck," and suddenly she was in a room with a video camera, and lights, and all these grownups she'd never seen before. She suddenly knew how a squirrel must feel in the sudden glare of a car's headlights.

"Hello, Kate. I'm Johnson Cormier, producer of *Backbeat*. This is Denise Lightstone, my partner and our main director. Colin, here, will be recording your reading on video so we can look back at it later. Have you ever been to an audition before?"

Still terrified, Kate shook her head. Mr. Cormier was imposing, wearing an expensive–looking suit, and a silk tie with Bugs Bunny on it. Kate thought the cartoon character was supposed to show that he was a regular guy, but it was too expensive to make *her* feel comfortable.

Mr. Cormier and the lady asked her a few questions. What school did she go to, did she have any brothers or sisters — that sort of thing. Answering them, she started to feel a bit better. She kind of liked the lady, who was in brown leggings and a beige summer sweater with a polished stone pendant in the shape of a doughnut. She was tugging at the pendant with long, elegant fingers that, to Kate's surprise, ended in fingernails that looked bitten. But she was still nervous. Then they asked her to read her part.

Kate cleared her throat, and took a breath. She had to remember not to talk too quickly, like everyone complained that she always did. She started. The part was of a kid who had been hauled into the principal's office for smoking in the washroom and was acting cocky and nervous about having been caught. Considering she felt kind of nervous already, Kate was able to get a pretty realistic tremor into her voice.

"Thank you, Kate," said Mr. Cormier. Then he glanced at the lady. (What was her name again?) Now what?

"Kate," said the director, fiddling with her pendant, "would you mind reading it again? Try to make it more defiant this time."

Oh, no. She'd done it wrong. She'd had too much nervous and not enough attitude in it. She breathed again. Tried to put an edge in her voice, control the nerves. When she was done, they didn't make any comments. Mr. Cormier just made a note on her application form, and then smiled coolly and said, "Thank you for your time. We'll be calling everyone on Friday to let you know whether or not you've been accepted for training."

"Thank you," said Kate, glad she'd remembered her manners. And that was that.

Two

On the bus on the way home, Kate and Maria compared notes.

"How do you think you did?" Kate asked, as the bus pulled away from the stop in front of Rolling Pictures.

"I'm not sure," Maria replied. "I thought I did okay, but then they asked me to do it over again."

"Me too." Kate felt glum.

"More snivelling," Maria explained.

Suddenly Kate brightened up. "Well, that's good then."

"Why?"

"Because they asked me to do it more defiant."

"I don't get it."

"Don't you see?" Kate pointed out. "They asked us to do different things — they were seeing if we could make it different."

"You think . . . ?" Maria brightened up too.

"Well," said Kate, her hopes sagging again, "maybe not. Maybe they were just giving us a second chance 'cause we blew the first one."

"Well, that's good." Maria sounded more cheerful now. "At least they didn't just go, 'Forget it,' right off the top."

For the next two days, Kate and Maria were both on pins and needles. They kept having the same conversation over and over. Kate thought being asked to read again was a good sign. On the hour, that is. Half an hour later, she was sure it was a bad sign, but by the time the next hour rolled around, she was certain it was good again. Maria seemed to be on the opposite schedule.

When they got tired of that conversation, they talked about the other actors auditioning. "Did you see that girl with the blonde hair?" Kate asked.

"Which one?" Maria replied. "There were so many."

"They're a dime a dozen," Kate said. "We'll stand out because we're different."

And Maria said, "Maybe. Do you think being asked to do it again was good?"

"No, it means we blew it," Kate answered.

"I don't think so," Maria shot back. "I think it's a good thing."

And round and round the conversation went.

Finally, it was Friday. Kate sat by the phone at her house, and she knew Maria must be doing the same thing at her place. The minutes went by even more slowly than they did in geography class when Mr. Horton snorted and honked his way through the lesson with a terrible headcold, making his drony voice even dronier — why on earth was she thinking about geography class when the phone could ring any minute and change her dull, meaningless life into an exciting, fantastic existence — but, on the other hand, it could ring and just prove to her what a dull, meaningless person she was, and she'd still be bored all summer . . .

The phone rang.

Kate jumped nearly out of her skin and grabbed the receiver.

"Hi, Kate. Did you hear anything yet?"

"Maria! Don't scare me like that. No, I haven't heard."

"When do you think they'll call?"

"Look, we can't gab — they might be trying to get through right now. I don't have call waiting — you know how my dad hates it."

"Okay," Maria said. "Good luck."

"Good luck yourself. Bye."

Kate put down the phone and willed it to ring again, but it didn't.

She wished she and Maria could be together. It seemed strange not to be together when something so important was going on. Kate and Maria knew everything about each other, did everything together. Maria was the only one in the world who knew about Kate's dad's moods and occasional black temper. And thanks to Kate, Maria had gotten her best science mark ever, on the cow project they had worked on last year — *and* they'd come second in the Science Fair. In the school yearbook, there had been a page of "Best Friends," and there were Maria and Kate together at the Science Fair with the cow project. They had written the same thing on each other's book, under the picture. "Make new friends, but keep the old. One is silver, and the other gold," and then stamped them with their camel rubber stamps. The camel was their secret code, from their initials, K.M. and M.L. They even greeted each other with a special wave, a curving arc that outlined the hump of a camel.

By now, Kate was going out of her mind. She couldn't sit still long enough to read, or even watch TV.

The phone rang.

Kate's heart started to pound.

This was it.

Her hands went cold.

She reached for the phone receiver and

·almost hesitated to pick it up.

The phone rang again.

Kate steadied herself.

"Merriman residence," she said into the receiver.

"Hello, Kate, it's Denise Lightstone." That was the lady with the pendant! "I'm calling to invite you to attend our training sessions. Of course . . . "

Kate cut her off with a whoop of elation.

"Heavens, you kids! I'm going to be deaf from making these calls!"

"Thank you thank you thank you, Ms. Lightstone. I'm so excited!"

"I just want to remind you that attending training does not guarantee you'll have a part on the show."

"That's okay. I'll work so hard . . . you'll see," Kate bubbled.

"And we'll need to speak to your parents. Could you ask them to call the office when they get in?"

"Yes!" exclaimed Kate.

"So we'll see you at our offices on Monday, then. Ten o'clock."

"I can't wait!"

As soon as she put the phone down, Kate whooped once more and then bolted out the door to Maria's house, three doors down.

She banged on the screen door when she got there and ran into Maria's living room,

leaping over scattered toys left by Maria's
little brothers and sisters. Maria was just
setting the receiver back down, turned and
screamed, "I made it!"

"So did I!" yelled Kate.

"We're in! We did it!" the two girls cried
out, as they hugged and leapt around the
room in a wild dance of joy.

• • •

The weekend crawled by. Maria managed
to talk Kate into going swimming on
Saturday, just for something to do, to make
the time pass. Kate wanted to paint designs
on herself with the lime–green zinc sunblock.
"Maybe people won't notice how pale I am,"
was her reasoning.

Maria managed to talk her out of it.
"Maybe people will notice how weird you are."
She rolled her eyes. "You and your crazy
ideas!"

At the pool, they lay on their towels and
daydreamed.

"Mmm . . . what do you suppose it will be
like?" Kate mused. She knew she didn't have
to explain to Maria what she was talking
about. She never did.

Maria was just as dreamy. "Who knows?"

"I think it will be like a ballet studio, with
mirrors all around. Will we have to dance?"

"Why would we have to dance?"

"I don't know." Kate rolled on her side to face her friend. "You know what? It's like *A Chorus Line* — remember? — they have all the people who want to get on the show, and they all have their own stories, and then only some of them get picked. I hope we get picked."

"I still like the guy who tap–danced," said Maria.

"I liked the Puerto Rican guy." It was an old argument. They grinned at each other. "Let's go home and listen to it," said Kate suddenly, jumping up.

Back at Kate's house, they put on the CD of *A Chorus Line*. They had pooled their money to buy it after going to see the show with Kate's parents last year, so it belonged to both of them. But it lived at Kate's house. At Kate's, there was more room to do the whole routine the girls had worked out, singing all the parts and dancing, complete with top hats and canes — or at least sun hats and wooden spoons from the kitchen. They had it all choreographed, from the opening song, "Hope I Get It" — which now took on new meaning for Kate — through "Hello, Twelve, Hello Thirteen" and "Dance Ten, Looks Three," which sent them into the giggles, to the final, high–kicking chorus line, as the music faded out.

Each girl had her own solo — Maria got "Nothing," and Kate's was "Kiss Today Goodbye." But their favourite song of all was "At the Ballet." In the chorus, they floated around the living room, waltzing together in a pas de deux.

On Sunday, Kate spent part of the afternoon examining herself in the full–length mirror behind her bedroom door. She could think of nothing but the exciting new life she was about to step into. How long would it last? Would she get a part? How would she look on camera? She noticed that she was getting freckles this year, and that the small crop of blackheads on her chin was almost gone. She also noticed that she might actually be sprouting something that, if she wanted to exaggerate, she might have called breasts. She made faces, to see what she looked like. After all, if she was going to be an actress, she had to be able to convey emotions. She tried a smile that she decided looked crazed, and an angry expression that was nearly murderous. She tried to look longing, then tragic, but they both looked kind of the same. She pulled her hair up on top of her head, for a sophisticated look, and decided her ears stuck out too much. She raked through her closets looking for something to wear on Monday. Ms. Lightstone had said to wear something comfortable that she didn't mind rolling around on the floor in. What on earth would they be rolling around on the floor for? She still wanted to look nice, especially if that really cute guy with the dark hair falling in his eyes was going to be there.

For the first time, she began wondering who else would be in the group, and she remembered all those gorgeous girls — who were probably fifteen — with the silky blonde hair. It didn't really matter much what she wore, because any cute guys who were there would be way more interested in them. So she decided to wear a pair of purple cycling shorts and a white T- shirt with the words "You Are Here" and a picture of the earth on it. And hot pink sneakers. And maybe her extra cool hat, the cloth one with the wide brim that folded up in front that was made of a patchwork of different colours of Indian cotton.

And where the heck was Maria? Her family Sunday dinner must be over by now.

Kate's family had been surprised when she had been accepted. Her mom had been thrilled ("Of course, you're our smart and beautiful Kate."). Her dad was a little skeptical at first ("Are they accepting just anyone?"), but when he was assured that it wasn't a trick to get them to pay for acting lessons or portfolios, he gave Kate a hug and said, "Good for you. That's my little girl."

"Kate! Maria's here!" called her mom from downstairs.

"In my room!" Kate shouted back. "Come on up!"

Maria came in, they gave a quick "camel wave," and then Maria flopped on Kate's bed, while Kate swung into the comfy chair with her legs over the back and her back on the seat.

"I'm so excited," bubbled Kate.

"Me too," Maria laughed, and they launched into the same conversation they had had six dozen times already since Friday.

"Suppose — just suppose — we pass the training, and we get a part," said Kate. "Do you think people will recognize us on the street? Will we have to get bodyguards? Will our pictures be in *Sixteen* and *Teen Beat*?"

"Of course!" Maria pretended she was reading from a magazine article. "Maria Lococco, star of *Backbeat*. Birthday: May nineteenth. Favourite colour: red. Favourite food: pizza. Favourite movie: *Beauty and the Beast*. Favourite books: Nancy Drew. Pet peeve: people who stick their gum under the desk top. Ambition: to be a famous clothing designer.'"

"'Kate Merriman, star of *Backbeat*.'" Kate used the same voice Maria had. "'Birthday: September first. Favourite colour: purple. Favourite food: artichokes. Favourite movie:

Beetlejuice. Favourite book: *Five Children and It*. Pet peeve: anything boring or ordinary. Ambition: to win an Oscar.'"

"Artichokes?" asked Maria. "You're weird."

"I just don't want to sound boring or ordinary," said Kate. "When I'm rich and famous, I'll buy all the artichokes I want. I'll buy the best clothes. Cowboy boots. I'll have a freezer full of Häagen Dazs Cookie Dough Dynamo ice cream. I'll have a chauffeured limo and a cook who makes the best onion rings in the world. I'll buy a house in Hollywood with a pool in the backyard and a built-in barbecue. And I'll go to parties with Tori Spelling. And you, of course."

"And I'll buy great clothes too, and some really cool art supplies, and I'll buy the house right next door to yours, with a tennis court. *I'll* go to parties with Keanu Reeves. And you. And . . . and . . . and . . . I'll have a pizza farm!"

They burst into a fit of the giggles, and after they'd laughed themselves into exhaustion, Kate swung around to sit in her chair the normal way. "Seriously, though," she said. "It's *tomorrow*. Aren't you sort of getting a little nervous? I mean, you saw all those kids at the audition. They looked like they knew what they were *doing*."

"Yeah, maybe a little nervous," Maria conceded.

THREE

By Monday morning, Kate was more than a little nervous. It was nine o'clock, and her parents had left for the office towers downtown where they worked — Mom usually dropped Dad off and then went to her accounting office near his.

"Break a leg," said Kate's mom.

"What?" asked Kate.

"It's a theatre thing. Actors say it's bad luck to say, 'Good luck,' so they say the opposite."

"Great, Mom." Kate rolled her eyes but submitted to her mom's hug. "Bye."

Maria would be coming over in a few minutes, and together they would take the bus to the offices of Rolling Films, not much more than fifteen minutes away. Kate had not been able to eat any cereal and had only just forced down a glass of juice and half a piece of toast. She wasn't even sure that would stay down. She felt like things were moving around under her skin, and even though it was quite warm out her hands were cold. Meanwhile, she could feel the sweat oozing from her underarms and went back into her room to put on another dose of deodorant. The doorbell rang.

As the girls waited for the bus, Kate turned to Maria. "You nervous?"

"Not really." Maria gave a nonchalant shrug of the shoulders and a tight grin. "You?"

"Nah." Kate tossed her head. If she was going to be an actress, she might as well start now.

They rode the bus in silence and arrived at Rolling Films with fifteen minutes to spare.

"Should we go in?" asked Maria.

"I don't know," said Kate. "We might look dumb if we're too early."

"Let's get a juice." Maria pointed to a doughnut shop across the street.

Kate shuddered at the thought of swallowing anything but said, "Okay."

They sat at a table in the window, in a spot where they could easily see the clock. "We'll go in at five to," said Kate.

"You know, Kate," said Maria, "I bet everyone else is just as new at this as we are almost. They wouldn't have picked us if they didn't think we could do it."

"I know," Kate replied. "And I can't imagine how nervous I'd be if I didn't have you with me. I just . . . well . . . " Kate let the sentence trail off. What she was thinking was how terribly important it had become to her to do well.

• • •

There were twenty kids in the group, ten girls and ten boys. Ms. Lightstone, today in turquoise leggings and a big white T-shirt with the stone pendant she had on before, had asked them all to call her Denise. The kids were all sitting on the carpeted floor, and Denise was explaining everything to them.

"We will be making six episodes of *Backbeat* during the fall," she said. "The network has agreed to air them and, based on the response, will decide whether to have us make more. The premise of the show is that the kids are all members of a garage band. *Backbeat* is different from a lot of shows because the kids are the main characters, not like in most sitcoms where the parents or teachers are the stars. And that's why we have these training sessions since very few of you have done any acting before. The training sessions are each morning for two weeks, then we'll have auditions for the five main characters."

Kate looked around the room. That meant fifteen wouldn't be cast. There were two tall blondes with silky hair, and the cute guy with the dark hair was there too. But not everybody was Hollywood gorgeous, so maybe that wasn't what they were looking for. A few kids were younger than her, some older, some her age — every shape and size and colour and type.

Denise was still talking. "That doesn't mean the rest of you won't get a chance to appear in an episode. There will be other parts for kids, and we'll cast first from amongst you, where possible. Now, let's get comfortable. Everybody lie down — we're going to get relaxed."

Once the relaxing exercise was over, Denise asked them to tell each other their names and one interesting thing about themselves. One of the blondes went first. She was wearing tight denim cutoffs and a small T-shirt that showed off her belly button, her great figure, and a lot of tanned skin .

"Hi, I'm Tawny Young," she said, dipping her head forward, so that her big silver hoops swung and her side-parted hair fell over her face. She unhitched one of her thumbs from her belt loop to brush it back. Kate took an instant dislike to this girl who was so perfect and seemed to know it. She literally looked polished. Her skin was perfect with a texture like silk, her teeth gleamed evenly, her hair was fine and satiny, and little bits of jewellery — even the button on her cutoffs — all shone. "Um . . . something interesting? Um . . . my mom and I went to India last winter, and we spent some time in an ashram." Tawny shrugged slightly and sat down.

In a what?

The cute boy turned out to be called John Pappas, and his father owned a lumber yard. There was also a tiny Chinese girl called Natalie, who got a laugh when she said she knew how to hula dance — and then gave a little demonstration.

Maria's interesting thing was that she liked to sew.

Kate was wracking her brains. She couldn't think of a single interesting thing about herself. Kate, who hated anything boring or ordinary, was boring and ordinary! She didn't even know what an ashram *was*.

It was her turn. "I'm Kate Merriman . . . and . . . um . . . I made an ashram in ceramics class once." Oh, no, what made her say that? It got a laugh, though, but Tawny pursed her lips.

"Ha–ha," said Denise, smiling. "Now tell us something real."

Halfway to sitting down again, Kate stood back up. "Uh . . . " she glanced at Maria. "My favourite food is artichokes," she blurted out and sat down. Even that comment brought smiles from the rest of the kids. Tawny rolled her eyes.

After introductions, Colin, the guy who had been working the camera at the audition, arrived and explained a whole bunch of technical stuff to them, most of which went over Kate's head. And then it was over. Denise told them to think of the most embarrassing thing that had ever happened to them for Wednesday, and then the kids dispersed, most going to one of the two bus stops in front of Rolling Films, a few leaving on bikes or on foot, or getting picked up in their parents' cars. Tawny was waiting for the same bus as Kate and Maria and was chatting with a girl with cascading red hair. " 'I made an ashram in ceramics class,' " the redhead mimicked Kate, just loud enough that Kate knew she was meant to overhear. "I bet she doesn't even know what an ashram is."

"Let's wait for the next bus," said Maria as a bus loomed into sight. "I think this bus will be too full — of snobs." She glanced back at the two older girls, just to make sure they'd heard.

"Maria . . . " muttered Kate. It was bad enough how things had started between her and Tawny, without making them worse.

But they took the next bus anyway.

• • •

By avoiding Tawny and the red–haired girl most of the time, Kate avoided having any more run–ins with them, and she and Maria started making friends with the rest of the kids in training. Kate especially liked Natalie's bubbly energy, and there was a kid called Zack who kept everyone in stitches with his wisecracks.

Kate also really liked Denise, probably most of all when she noticed that Denise's fingers would sometimes drift towards her mouth, and then she'd catch herself and start playing with the stone pendant instead. Kate had complimented her on the stone — it was deep brown, with golden stripes deep inside it. Denise told her it was called a "soothing stone," a tiger–eye.

Training was both fun and awful. They had to tell their most embarrassing moments while standing in funny positions. It was sup-posed to free them from self–consciousness, Denise said. They had to do an exercise where they fell and other people caught them, to get them to learn to trust each other, Denise said. They had to say silly lines in dif-ferent voices, to help them use their voices in different ways, Denise said. They had to do tongue twisters, to help them pronounce words clearly and not talk too fast, Denise said. This turned out to be the biggest problem for Kate.

Maria blushed all the way through her embarrassing moment, and really couldn't let herself fall on the others. But she could say, "As one black bug bled blue–black blood, the other black bug bled blue," as Kate could not. Kate could stand in any silly position, say any silly thing, fall anywhere, but could not get that sentence out without at least one "black blug" in it.

"Slow down, Kate," encouraged Denise. "There's no rush. The point of this is not to say it fast, it's to say it clearly."

"As ... one ... black ... bug! Bled blue–black ... blood! The other ... black ... bug! Bled blue."

"Good girl!" said Denise. "Now try it a little more like a real sentence."

"As one black bug ... " Kate hesitated. She'd made the first bug. Denise nodded. "Bled blue–black blood, the other black blug . . . oh rats!" snapped Kate in frustration.

"It's okay, love," soothed Denise. "Practise it at home — you'll soon get it."

On the bus, Kate complained to Maria, "I don't see why we have to do the stupid black blug thing — I mean, are all our lines going to be tongue twisters? I hope not."

"It's just to get us to slow down and speak clearly," said Maria. "It's not real lines."

"I know," sighed Kate as she looked out the bus window.

Maria put her hands beside her temples, extending her index fingers like a pair of antennae and wiggling them. "When it's real lines, and you're going too fast, I'll do this," she offered. "That'll remind you about the black bug, and you'll slow down."

Kate laughed in spite of herself and put her fingers up for antennae, wiggling them. "I've got the 'acting bug'," she announced.

● ● ●

The next morning at training, Denise announced that they should begin thinking of which part they wanted to audition for.

"It doesn't matter which role you audition for," she explained. "Mr. Cormier and I will put you in the part that we feel you are best suited to. However, you should work to your strengths. Who do you feel you are most like? What type of role do you think you could bring humanity and complexity to in each episode? We'd like you to devise your own costume. When you come into the room, you are in character throughout. That means that, in addition to your monologue, you answer any questions in character, you *are* that character until you leave the room."

As Denise handed out several sheets of

paper, the room was buzzing. What characters would there be? Kate wondered which part would be best for her.

The first three sheets were boy characters, and the second two were girls, one called Sassy, the other Diana. "That's not fair," whispered Maria to Kate. "There's only two parts for girls, but the boys get to choose from three."

Kate had to agree. But Denise was calling for their attention.

The kids were divided into smaller groups, and each of them read each part, boy or girl. Tawny was in Kate's group, and Kate thought she read Sassy especially well. Sassy was the lead singer in the garage band, and, according to the sheet, her name was appropriate. She was outspoken, fun–loving, and . . . well, sassy. Diana was the bass player, sophisticated, quieter, and more serious.

It was Kate's turn to read Sassy. The monologue had a change in mood part way through, which some kids had made too jarring, Kate thought. She didn't think that, in the length of one monologue, a person's mood would change totally. She tried to find what was the same in the two moods and decided it was Sassy's bravado. Whatever she was saying, she was saying it to impress someone; she was always thinking of her audience and how she was being seen. That was what

Tawny had been able to do with her reading, and it was what Kate was trying to do.

" . . . a'course, at's not why'm telling you this . . . " Kate was saying, when out of the corner of her eye she caught Maria wiggling her fingers — the blue black bug. Sharply, Kate slowed down, and backtracked in the monologue. "That's not why I'm telling you this at all," she continued. Thank goodness for Maria. Where would she be without her?

The readings went on until everyone had read all the parts. The group leaders — in Kate's case, Denise — gave them each some feedback on their reading, and then they were dismissed for the day.

The would–be actors had taken to hanging out for a few minutes after training around the front door of the office. Today no one was leaving early.

"Who are you auditioning for?"

"I don't know yet. What about you?"

"Well, I haven't decided. Say, who are you going out for?"

Everyone wanted to know who the others were trying out for, but no one wanted to reveal their own secrets.

• • •

That afternoon, Kate and Maria were walking to art class together. It was held at the community centre, where the swimming pool was.

"Have you decided yet who you're going to audition for?" asked Maria.

"I think Sassy," said Kate. After all, you have to tell your best friend. "What about you?"

"Not sure yet," replied Maria.

Kate stopped on the sidewalk and turned to her friend. "Come on, you have to tell!"

"It's not that," said Maria — a little crossly, Kate thought. "I'm just not quite decided."

They walked on. "I mean," Kate mused, "I figure, if Sassy's the lead singer in the band, it's probably the main role, and it'd be neat to be the star. But on the other hand, probably everyone's going out for Sassy because of that — but still, I don't think I'm the cool, sophisticated type like Diana, do you? You could play Diana."

"Hm . . . " was Maria's only reply, as they arrived at the art class.

After class, Kate took it up again. "Come on, Maria, you have to tell me — or at least go for Diana. We can't be against each other if we both want to get on the show. Go for Diana, and I'll go for Sassy. You'll probably be the only one going for Diana anyway, and then you'll get on, and I won't, which would be terrible, I guess — but at least if one of us gets the part, it won't be because we beat each other."

"Denise said it didn't matter which parts we went for — they'll decide anyway," replied Maria.

"Oh, right . . . you believe that? I mean, if I go in there and try to convince them I'm Sassy, they'd never believe I could do Diana. We have to try for the right ones."

Maria didn't say anything.

"Okay, then, I'll go for Diana . . . you go for Sassy," Kate continued after a short silence. "Really, the worst thing that could happen would be if one of us beat the other one out. After all, best friends are best friends."

Maria smiled at her. That was better.

"But I think you'd make a better Diana than I would," finished Kate. "And really, don't you think I'm more of a Sassy?"

"I kind of wanted to go for Sassy," admitted Maria. "But you're right. We can't go for the same part. I'll go for Diana."

"Oh, yes!" cried Kate, as much in relief as anything else. "It'll be so perfect! You'll be Diana, I'll be Sassy, we'll be stars together — Hollywood, here we come!"

FOUR

That evening, after dinner, Kate began looking through her wardrobe for a Sassy costume. She felt a little guilty. Had she bullied Maria into trying for Diana? Yet she was right — she knew she was — that Maria was more like Diana, and she was more like Sassy. No depth. That was her problem. Kate could kick herself sometimes. Sometimes her mouth got ahead of her brain, and she forgot that other people might have their own opinions of things. Still, she knew she was right. Then again, probably neither one of them would be cast. Look at Tawny, her friend Aimee, some of the other gorgeous girls in the training. They'd probably get the main parts. Kate sighed. What was the point, really? She looked at her purple bicycle shorts. Would they make a good Sassy? Maybe. Was there a point? Yes, there was. The point was, Kate loved acting. Sure, she'd had fun being a pirate in *Peter Pan*, but this was real. This was motivation and technique and diction and . . . well, it was real acting, not just school plays, and she was pretty good at it, too, she thought. But then, so was practically everyone in the training.

What would Sassy wear for a top? Kate pulled her T–shirt tight behind her and looked at her profile in the mirror. Sassy would probably wear something sexy, a halter maybe — except Kate figured she would look like she had on a surgical mask that had slipped. Or a cropped T–shirt like Tawny wore. Kate hauled out an old top from a bottom drawer and took a pair of scissors to it. She cut off nearly the entire bottom half, and tried it on. Looking in the mirror, she made a face. Somehow, she looked more like a little kid who'd outgrown her clothes than a sexy lead singer in a band. And that was really the problem. She looked like a little kid.

Kate flopped down in her chair, grabbed her Gameboy and began to play Tetris as she thought about the part. How could she have thought she should go out for the part of Sassy? Maybe she should try for Diana — call Maria, and tell her she could have Sassy. But then she thought, if I can't do sexy Sassy, how could I ever do sophisticated Diana? But they were her only choices.

Kate thought about the last time she'd had to come up with a costume. It was the cow project, of course, when she'd had the crazy idea of she and Maria dressing up as beef and dairy cattle. That was probably what had won them second prize in the Science Fair, because it was just so outrageous. And also because of the way it worked, and the information. There was a board, and visitors to the display could press a button next to each part, like "horns," and Kate's dad had helped them rig up Christmas lights so that when you pressed "horns," a light on their horns would come on. Kate and Maria had cards about each of the parts, and they would read out about the horns of the dairy and beef cattle. Kate was a Holstein, and Maria was an Aberdeen Angus. Maria had done a lot of the sewing, and Kate had done the research and written out the cards. She and her dad had spent hours in the basement workshop together, figuring out how to get the lights rigged properly and attaching them inside the costumes. And when the judges placed them in the medals, Kate had almost burst with pride that one of her crazy ideas had actually worked.

Still, Sassy was not a cow. Just the opposite, in fact. What about doing Sassy not so much sexy, but kind of cute and perky, maybe will–be–sexy, maybe wishes–she–were–sexy–now, maybe thinks–she's–sexy? Kate started to smile. That was a way to do it. Bicycle shorts — sure. Peasant blouse pulled off the shoulders. The puffiness would hide what she didn't have anyway. And Sassy would know a thing like that. Kate thought back to the reading that morning. Hadn't she seen Sassy as all show, doing it for the audience? Then she'd know how to seem sexy even if she had nothing on top. A little too much makeup. Big hair. Kate teased her already curly hair a little. Pity she wasn't quite blonde — but oh, well. Shoes with a little heel. This was starting to work. Kate examined herself in the mirror. Put on a locket. Put on a few bangles — not too many, she's not supposed to look like a kid dressed up in her mother's clothes. She's supposed to look like she knows what she's doing. Kate stood looking in the mirror, popped a piece of bubble gum in her mouth. Chewed with her mouth open. "I'm not trying to make anybody mad or anything." Kate began the monologue. It flowed. It worked. Kate had become Sassy.

Finally it was audition day. Maria called for Kate as usual, on her way to the bus stop. Kate was in her purple bicycle shorts and peasant blouse, which she still had up on her shoulders — she didn't dare appear so trampy in public, her mother would have had a fit, and Kate wouldn't have felt that comfortable anyway. She already felt a bit trashy with the teased hair and extra makeup.

The jewellery was in her bag. She'd put it on when she got to the office. She greeted Maria with a quick camel wave, and Maria camel–waved back.

Maria was wearing a short, pleated skirt and a hot pink tank top with a man's jacket and white platform hi–tops. Kate thought Maria's costume was a bit odd for the part of Diana, but she didn't say anything. A little too floozy–ish for the supposedly sophisticated Diana, though the man's jacket was the right touch. Still, she supposed Maria had her own idea of Diana.

"Nervous?" asked Maria, as they waited for the bus.

"Not really. Excited, more." Kate bounced on the balls of her feet. "Keyed up, but in a good way. What about you?"

"I'm . . . okay," replied her friend. "I'll do my best . . . and if I don't get the part . . . well, I don't, I figure."

"Denise did say they'd be casting other parts from the rest of us," said Kate as the bus huffed to a stop. "Even if we don't get Sassy and Diana, we might get something else, you know."

"That's right," agreed Maria, as they boarded the bus and paid their fares. Somehow, Kate felt her friend was distant. Not really distant — she couldn't quite put her finger on it — more . . . *detached*, that was a better word. Kate herself was telling the truth when she said she was keyed up, but in a good way. She knew her part — had gone over it a zillion times with her parents. They had approved her costume (" . . . but don't let me catch you in public in it," her dad warned her, half–jokingly). They had asked her some questions which she tried to answer in character. It had been a fun evening.

"I've done some theatrics, myself, you know," said Kate's dad in a jokey–pompous voice. "The audience wept in my death scene in Julius Caesar. Unfortunately, it was tears of laughter."

Kate's mom had obviously heard the story before, because she started smiling even before her dad started telling it. Kate looked at her dad quizzically.

"I had a couple of longish speeches before the death," he explained, "and I managed to get through them. Then there's a bit of back and forth. My last line was: 'Doth not Brutus bootless kneel?' — and it came out, 'Dot noth brutnus brutnus kneel?' Next, the guys all had to kill me — they had their backs to the audience, and they all started to laugh, and I'm supposed to be dead, covered in fake blood. They managed to get through their lines, but I had to lie dead on stage for the rest of the scene, and the more I thought about it, the more I laughed, and the audience could see my chest going up and down, and they started to laugh, and it just made me laugh more. By the time this incredibly serious scene was over, hardly any of the actors could squeak out their lines. I'm telling you — once we finally got off-stage, the guys were ready to kill me for real."

Kate could just see her dad doing something like that in his university days, and the image made her laugh so hard her sides were hurting. At least she wasn't the only actor in the family who couldn't say tongue-twisters. She thought about her audition the next day (The Next Day!)

"Do you think there's a chance I might get it?" Kate asked.

Her parents exchanged a glance. "I think you're very good," said her mom. "But who knows what they're looking for?"

"You've worked really hard at this," commented her dad. "You deserve it. But like your mom said . . . "

Both had wished her luck and told her not to be too disappointed if she didn't get the part — she'd still learned a lot, and she was their smart and beautiful, and Dad's little, and blah blah blah — but Kate knew the part was hers. She burned with it.

Kate and Maria arrived at the Rolling Films office with time to spare and sat down in the plushy gray chairs. The office didn't intimidate her any more, she'd been here so many times. The lady with the trendy glasses dressed in black was now Holly, and she said "Hi" when they came in.

All the girls from training were sitting around the room, gabbing — probably, like Kate, trying not to think too hard about the auditions. It was obvious by the array of sexy outfits that nearly all of them were going for Sassy. She felt sick in the pit of her stomach. Why hadn't she gone for Diana? She could never compete in this crowd. Still, can't let them know. Sassy wouldn't.

"Hi, Sassies," greeted Kate, brazenly.

"Hi, Sassy," said Natalie, the youngest in the crowd.

"Is *anyone* going for Diana?" another girl asked.

"I am," said Tawny. They all looked at her. She was dressed in black from head to toe — in fact Kate thought she looked more like she was going out for Holly's job. Black leggings, black Doc Marten boots, a black tank top, and a black denim jacket were topped with a multi– coloured, Kente cloth pillbox that beautifully set off her blonde hair.

It was only later that Kate realized that she'd been so amazed by Tawny's outfit that she hadn't noticed Maria's silence.

Natalie was wearing a strange getup. She

had on baggy jeans and a big baggy T-shirt, and her usual long ponytail was tucked through the back of a baseball cap. If that was her idea of Sassy . . . . Kate looked at the other six Sassy hopefuls. Some were good, some not so good. But hers was the best, she was certain of it.

One by one, the girls were called in. As each was called, she made some small adjustment to her costume, straightened her shoulders, and went through to the office where they had originally auditioned.

"Maria, go on in," said Holly, as Natalie came out grinning.

Kate spent the whole time Maria was out of the room with her fingers crossed. It would be so cool if both of them got parts.

It seemed like only seconds before Maria returned, smoothing her hair and smiling. She cracked her gum. "I knocked 'em dead, babe," she joked to Kate. Before Kate had a chance to ask what kind of questions they asked her, she herself was called into the office. Just like the others she stood up, then puffed her hair, pulled the peasant blouse off her shoulders, straightened her posture, and sashayed into the audition room.

"Hi, Kate," said Denise. "You remember Mr. Cormier, Colin." She pointed at each of them.

"Hi, guys," said Kate, much more forwardly than Kate ever would. But it was Sassy talking. She couldn't believe how brazen she was being — and how easily it came. She stood with her hand on her hip and her chin slightly down, so she had to kind of roll her eyes up to see them. She cracked her gum.

Denise smiled slightly and took her hand away from her pendant. "Won't you take a seat, Sassy?" she asked.

But Kate had rehearsed her monologue standing. She had worked out all the moves and gestures.

"S'okay fie stand?" she asked, and suddenly, unbidden, she had an image in her mind of Maria miming the little bug at her. Probably she was sending it to her telepathically. She slowed down. Thank heaven for Maria, even when she wasn't there. "I mean, like, I've been sitting down on that stupid school bus all day. I'm not trying to make anybody *mad* or anything . . . " And Kate launched into her monologue.

It wasn't bad. It wasn't bad at all. She remembered her lines, remembered the bits of "business" — little actions to make the character seem like a real person, to show the audience a little more of who she was — that she had worked out. But it wasn't brilliant. She knew herself that she'd made the mood change a little too big. It wasn't awful.

But it wasn't great.

"Thank you, Kate," said Denise when she'd finished. "We'll call you by Friday and let you know what's happening."

"Okay," said Kate, still in character, and turned to leave the room. But she couldn't quite not say thank you. It was just a little too rude, and she didn't want Denise to think that Kate wouldn't say thank you, even if Sassy wouldn't. Just as she was about to close the door, she turned and said it. "Thank you." Just like Kate would.

• • •

Again, time crept by at an imperceptible pace. Kate tried to pass the time by reading or watching TV or whatever. The ticking of the clock on the dining room sideboard sounded more like someone trying to fell a redwood with a hatchet. It was loud, it was rhythmically incessant, but it wasn't making much of a dent.

Oddly, Maria didn't want to talk about the audition at all. Every time Kate tried to get her to do the game of what they would say about themselves in the teen magazines, or of how great their lives would be once they were big stars, Maria changed the subject.

"I don't want to do that," she'd say. "We've done it enough."

"But it's fun to imagine," Kate would argue.

"The audition's over. There's nothing we can do now, just wait."

And wait. And wait.

• • •

It was Friday. Kate, going mad all alone in her house, tried to read a book, tried to do a crossword, tried to teach herself to knit from a book, just to take her mind off things. But it was impossible. She wanted that part so badly. She wanted so badly to act. She told herself: if she didn't get this one there might be other chances. But not this chance. How often did people make television shows here in Lakeview? Or movies either?

Imagine if she did get the part. Life would be so different. She and Maria — for surely, Maria would get Diana — would be recognized on the street, they'd have to go to shopping malls and give autographs. And they'd be acting every day, breathing life into characters who wouldn't exist until they gave them shape and form and personality. Kate would be an actress.

Finally, Kate made herself so dizzy with nerves and imagining and excitement that she put on some of her mom's exercise tapes, one after another, and did exercises along with them. It didn't take her mind off anything, but at least it got rid of some of the excess energy.

The phone rang. Kate's stomach flipped over so abruptly she thought she might throw up.

This was it.

The beginning of a life of stardom.

Or the end of life as we know it on this planet.

"Merriman residence," said Kate, her heart pounding.

"Hello, Kate, it's Denise Lightstone. I'm sorry it's taken so long to call. It has been quite a difficult decision we have had to make."

Get on with it, get on with it.

"As you know, we only had two parts for girls at this point."

Kate felt hope slither away like water through a cupped hand.

"We were very impressed with your audition, however, and we are placing you high on our preferred casting list."

"Okay," said Kate, dully.

"Please don't feel disappointed," said Denise, her voice gentle. "I'm certain we will have a role for you soon — if you're still interested."

"Oh, yes, I'm still interested," Kate replied, trying to put as much enthusiasm in her voice as she could manage.

"Good. I'm sure we'll be talking again soon then, love," finished Denise.

"Thanks, Denise."

"Goodbye for now."

"Bye."

Kate set the receiver slowly back into its cradle. She had thought, if she didn't get the part, she might cry. But she just mainly felt numb. She slumped down on the sofa. On the TV screen, some chirpy female was cooing, "Yew can dew it! Come on! Four more, three more, two more . . . " Kate picked up the zapper and cut her off.

Still feeling numb, Kate rewound the tape, slowly got up, and put it away in its box. Maria! They must have called Maria by now. It would be awful to say that she didn't want Maria to get the part of Diana. But right now, she just didn't want to *hear* that Maria had gotten the part. Art class was this afternoon. That was soon enough.

The phone rang again. Kate hesitated to pick it up, in case it was Maria with her own good news, but after a ring she reached for it. It turned out to be her mom.

"Has the film company called?" she asked.

"Yeah," said Kate. "They put me on 'preferred casting'."

"Well, that's good, isn't it?"

"I guess so."

"You're still my wonderful girl," Mom said.

Kate smiled a little, but she wondered whether her dad would actually say "I told you so," or only think it. Or whether he'd be secretly relieved.

"And you never know what this 'preferred casting' list might mean," her mom was saying.

"Yeah." Kate's voice was unenthusiastic. She knew her mom was saying all the right things, but Kate wasn't quite ready to hear them yet.

• • •

At one, Kate knocked on Maria's screen door. She didn't go flying into the house this time, like she had before. When Maria came to the door, she looked subdued, giving a lifeless camel wave.

"Did you hear anything?" she asked Kate.

Kate nodded glumly. "I'm on 'preferred casting'." she told her.

"Me too," shrugged Maria.

A little glimmer of light appeared in Kate's world. It wasn't that she'd wanted her friend to fail. But it was nice not to be alone.

The two walked to art class without saying much.

"Do you think preferred casting means anything?" Kate asked at one point.

"Who knows?" replied Maria, and the girls walked on in silence.

Arriving in the art studio, the girls set up their easels and got out their charcoal in preparation for class. A girl called Shaylene waved to Maria.

"Oh," said Maria, reaching into her bag. "Here are your earrings back. Thanks."

"No prob," replied Shaylene. "Did you get the part?"

Maria shook her head sadly. But Kate was puzzled. The earrings were big beaded things, with brightly coloured beads spraying out in all directions. Why would Maria have borrowed them? And why did Shaylene ask about the part? And why did the earrings look sort of familiar? Someone cracked their gum, and the sound reminded Kate of something. Maria had cracked gum when she came out of the audition. And she had been wearing those earrings. She wasn't wearing them when she went into the audition. She wasn't wearing them on the bus on the way home. And she hadn't spoken up when Natalie had asked who was going for Diana. The gum, the earrings, the odd costume, the smoothing back of her hair, the non–answer, Maria's coolness. It was like something in a dream where you open a strange door and realize you're home. But not so happy a thought.

"Maria," said Kate, quietly. "You auditioned for Sassy, didn't you?"

The guilty look on Maria's face was the clearest answer she could give.

FIVE

Class began before Kate had a chance to figure out what she wanted to say, which was probably just as well. Knowing herself, she figured she would have blurted out some awful thing and felt terrible afterwards. This way, she had the whole class to stew through.

At first she was really angry at Maria for breaking the agreement that they wouldn't compete against each other. But then she remembered that that was only her idea, and that Maria hadn't seemed too convinced. She leaned back and had a look at her drawing. She really wasn't very good. They were doing an exercise in perspective, learning about converging lines and vanishing points. She was okay at the perspective part, but her fence posts looked like they were made of plasticene — there was no life, no reality to them. Perspective. Neither one of them had gotten the part anyway, so maybe it didn't make any difference. Maybe it was best just to forget about the whole thing, since it was kind of irrelevant anyway.

After class, Kate put away her supplies without looking at Maria. She felt Maria should come to *her*, since she was the one at fault, but Kate knew that she was ready to forgive her friend already.

Maria was cheerily chatting with Shaylene, apparently not laden down under a burden of massive guilt. When everything was put away and cleaned up, Maria said goodbye to Shaylene and came to join Kate.

"Ready to go?" Maria asked her.

"Yeah," replied Kate, trying not to show how betrayed she felt.

They walked along for a bit, and Kate was starting to get mad again. Maria could at least have apologized!

"You're awfully quiet," said Maria.

Kate looked at her.

"You're not mad about me going for Sassy, are you?" asked Maria, obviously surprised.

"I thought we agreed," said Kate.

"Well, yeah . . . but it doesn't matter, does it? Neither of us got the part."

"But what if we had?" was Kate's reply.

"But we didn't," argued Maria.

"Still . . . I thought we agreed," said Kate.

The girls walked in silence for a few more minutes. Kate wasn't quite so ready to forgive her friend any more. If she'd just apologize . . .

A few moments later, Maria said, "Look, I'm sorry I made you mad. I don't think it's that big a deal, but I didn't mean to cause trouble."

"Well, why didn't you tell me then," asked Kate, "if it's not such a big deal?"

Maria looked down at the ground. "I guess I knew you'd make a fuss." She looked up at Kate. "You do get a hold of things in your mind sometimes, you know."

Kate felt surprised. She didn't think she was all that stubborn, as Maria was suggesting, but what they had agreed on made sense; they shouldn't have been competing for the same part. But at least Maria had apologized. She should let this go now.

"Sorry for making a fuss," she said. "Friends?"

"Friends," said Maria. "Anyway, it's a dumb show. It'll never get on TV."

"But Denise said . . . " Kate began to protest.

"What do you *think* she'd say?" Maria anticipated her. "They're not a *real* film company. If they were, they'd be in Hollywood, or New York . . . not Lakeview."

"I guess so," Kate replied, but she wasn't convinced.

• • •

The next morning, Kate woke up with a gloomy feeling, a feeling that something was wrong. Then she remembered. She hadn't got the part. She was off the show. She moped around the house all morning, played Tetris till she got bored, then Maria called her to go swimming in the afternoon. It turned out to be a good thing to do — the water was refreshing, and it was good just to do something, just to move around and forget about her disappointment. Kate and Maria giggled over the cute new lifeguard, and talked about high school in the fall and about whether there would be any cute boys there.

"For sure!" said Maria, emphatically. "There'll be guys who are, like, eighteen."

"Who won't pay the slightest bit of attention to us," Kate reminded her.

"Maybe not the eighteen–year–olds . . . " Maria conceded.

Eventually, it was time to go home, but Kate was feeling way better than she had since Denise's phone call. Somehow, sharing the misery with her best friend made it easier to take.

Thinking about Denise's phone call made her a little blue, but Kate realized she was already feeling better about everything. She was even feeling a little curious as to who *did* get the part of Sassy — and all the others, of course. Well, she'd probably have to wait to see it on television to find out.

Kate was first home — her parents would be in from work shortly, her dad from the law office, and her mom from a client meeting. She got the mail, which was all just boring stuff for her parents, and went to check the answering machine. There were two messages.

The first one was just someone hanging up, but the voice on the second one was familiar.

"Hi, Kate, it's Denise. Well, I didn't expect to be calling you so soon, but we've got the script for the first episode, and we have a small part for you if you're still interested. Please get back to me at . . . "

Kate's whoop drowned out the telephone number, but she knew it by heart anyway. Even a small part would get her on the show, and maybe they'd like her. Maybe they'd have the small part again. As long as her character didn't get killed in the opening scene — which didn't seem very likely for a kids' show — she'd take it.

Kate dialed the number right away.

"Rolling Films, good afternoon," came the voice.

"Holly . . . hi, it's me, Kate Merriman! Denise said to call!"

Holly laughed. "Calm down! Denise is out scouting locations right now. Did she call you about a small part?"

"Yes!" Kate practically yelled.

"I take it that means you are interested," teased Holly.

"Yes! Yes!" exclaimed Kate.

"Now it's just a small part, just a couple of lines," cautioned Holly. "You'd be playing a paper girl."

"I don't care . . . anything is fine with me," replied Kate.

"Okay. Can you come down next Thursday for a script read–through? In the afternoon . . . two o'clock."

Thursday afternoon was art class, but who cared? She could skip.

"I'll be there," Kate assured her. "Do I need to bring anything?"

"Nothing but your talent and a great attitude," said Holly.

As soon as she hung up, she called Maria, but Maria's older sister Luisa answered.

"You're on call waiting," she said. "She'll call you back." Hanging up, Kate realized she didn't quite know what to tell her friend. What if Maria hadn't been called too? She didn't want to make Maria feel bad, but she was dying to tell her about her exciting news. She decided just to tell her in a casual kind of way.

When Maria called back, Kate answered on the first ring.

"Oh . . . hi, Maria," said Kate. "I just got a phone call from Denise."

"Me too," Maria replied.

Yay! It was okay to be elated!

"Aren't you excited?" bubbled Kate. "I mean it's only a small part — mine is anyway — but we'll get to be on the show and everything! What part are you getting?"

"They said the younger sister of Bryce. But I said no," said Maria, in a calm voice.

"Did you say you turned it down?!" Kate was flabbergasted. "Why?"

"The rehearsal thing is at the same time as art class."

"So? We can skip," argued Kate.

"I don't want to skip," was Maria's response. "Besides, it's not just one time. We'd probably have to miss for filming and everything too. I didn't want to, just for one line."

"But a kid sister — that could be a big, recurring role. I'm just a paper girl — I might only be on the one time."

"It's just a rinky–dink show," said Maria. "It's not worth it."

Why was Maria so down on the show? Why couldn't Kate convince her to change her mind? She heard the front door close and quickly hung up. Her parents were excited when they heard the news. Her dad hadn't said, "I told you so," when she didn't get the

part in the first place, but Kate could tell
that he was surprised now. As he went to
pour his customary after–work Scotch on the
rocks, a sudden little flicker of irritation at
her father — why should he be surprised that
Kate had succeeded? — was washed away in
her mom's excitement and effusive praise.

By the time they were all sitting at dinner, though, her dad had come around, and
he was as full of excitement and speculation
as Kate and her mom.

Kate could barely contain herself until
Thursday. She and Maria did their usual
stuff together, but they didn't talk about the
show. Kate wanted to speculate with her
friend as to who would have the main roles,
but the whole topic seemed better left alone.
It was a strain, not being able to talk with
her best friend about the most exciting thing
that had ever happened to her. But it might
have upset Maria to talk about it, and Kate
understood that best friends knew when to
back off.

Finally the day came. Kate decided she
wanted to look nice. She put on her favourite
skirt, purple Indian cotton with yellow stars
and gold trim, sandals, and a plain yellow
T–shirt. At last it was late enough to go and
get the bus. It felt strange, going to Rolling
Films by herself without Maria. But it felt
exciting and very grown up too.

When she arrived at the office, Holly sent her into the same room where she had auditioned. The big table, which had been to one side before, was now in the middle, and there were twelve chairs around it, some of them empty and some of them occupied. John Pappas was there, and they said "Hi" to each other. A woman Kate had not seen before was there too, and she gave Kate a small smile. Zack, the boy who was always wisecracking in training, was across from where she sat down, and they waved to each other. Kate felt very shy. It seemed strange that Maria wasn't here with her — after all, trying out for *Backbeat* had been Maria's idea in the first place.

Just then, Natalie and another of the younger kids called Brooke came in together, and hi's were exchanged. After them came Tawny and Aimee, quickly followed by Denise, today in cherry pink top and leggings, with her constant soothing stone, and Mr. Cormier, as always in a double-breasted suit, along with a man Kate did not know, who was in jeans and a T-shirt and wore a beard.

"Oh good, you're all here," said Denise, taking a place at one end of the table. "Some of you have met, I know, but let me go around and make introductions. You all know me, Denise Lightstone. This is Mr. Cormier, of

61

course, and this is Larry Kessler, our story editor and main writer." Denise indicated the man with the beard. Kate thought it was kind of odd how his hair was dark with gray sprinkled throughout but his beard was almost red. Denise was still talking. "Around the table . . . Sharla James, who'll be playing B.B.'s mother . . . John is Bryce." So Maria would have played John's sister. Too bad for her. "Brooke has a small role as River." Everyone laughed. "Natalie is Georgie — formerly George — Zack is B.B., Kate is the paper girl, Julie."

Kate glanced to her left as Denise went on. "And Aimee is Diana, and, of course, Tawny is Sassy. Here are your scripts. Shall we begin?"

SIX

Kate took the script Denise handed to her. She couldn't believe she was holding an actual, real script for TV — one that practically no one in the world had seen yet.

It turned out that Julie had four lines. Kate planned to have them memorized by the time she got home. They were: "Here's your paper, Mr. Simpson," "You guys are starting a band?" "Could I join?" and "No," — the last in answer to whether Julie played an instrument. But the neat part was that even though she only spoke in two scenes, she actually had a lot to do, because she spent the rest of the episode spying on the band's rehearsals.

The read–through was interesting, each person reading out their own part. You could sort of see how the show would come together. Everyone flubbed at least one of their lines, so nobody felt completely stupid, and they all started to feel kind of together as a group, except that Kate was still intimidated by Tawny and Aimee. She might have known the gorgeous ones would get the big parts.

They didn't do much to make her feel at home either. Aimee was sort of flirting with Larry, who wrote notes and chewed on his pen all the way through the read–through, and Tawny was sucking up to Denise and Mr. Cormier. Aimee had really gorgeous, long, curly red hair, and she knew it. She kept twirling a piece of it around her finger, and kind of looking out from under her eyelashes with those incredible turquoise eyes. Tawny, meanwhile, looked anxiously at Denise after every line she delivered, as if checking to see if she was doing it right. Denise, Kate noticed, didn't respond to that, but just kept fingering her soothing stone as she followed along in the script.

Kate saw the name "Julie" coming up in the next scene. This was her first line.

"Here's yr paper Misimpson," she blurted out. Well, that wasn't very good. Suddenly she remembered Maria's dying bug. She could see her friend wiggling her fingers like antennae beside her temples. Well, okay: she'd do the next line better.

It came quite soon, in the very next scene. "Yooo guys are star–ting a band?" Oh no, now she was over–enunciating!

"Yeah," said Zack, as B.B., brightly. "We're calling ourselves 'The Garage Band'."

"Could I join?" said Kate, as Julie. Well,

that was better.

"Do you play an inst . . . instrument?" asked John, playing Bryce.

"No," said Kate, trying to sound dejected.

"Forget it, then," said Tawny, very Sassy–like.

Then the stage directions called for Julie to leave sadly, but since they weren't acting it out yet, Kate didn't. Throughout the rest of the story, which was about the beginnings of the band and the trouble they have getting started, Kate's character was seen peering through the garage window, hiding behind bushes, and so on. But she didn't have any more lines.

After the read–through, Denise told them how terrific they all were, and everybody said how much they liked the script. Then they were told to check with Holly about when they would be doing costume stuff. Kate's appointment was Thursday, so she'd have to miss another art class — but so what? This was the Big Time! It was just like Hollywood, but right here in Lakeview.

As she rode home on the bus, Kate was on another planet. She imagined a big sign in square white letters suspended somewhere above the city — there were no hills to put it on — saying *LAKEVIEW*. She imagined herself in sunglasses, and instead of riding on the bus, she was being driven in a chauf-

feured limousine — not because she was a
snob, but because she couldn't go anywhere
without being recognized, and sometimes she
needed her privacy. She imagined arriving
home to sit on a lawn chair by the pool that
would take up most of the back yard, someone bringing her champagne on a silver tray.
The sun would always be shining, and it
would be warm enough for palm trees, even
in February — which was obviously ridicu-
lous in this part of the world, but it was fun
to think about.

Back in the real world, Kate thought
about the script. Denise had said that there
might be some changes to it before they filmed
it, so they weren't allowed to keep the scripts,
or even tell other people what it was about —
except their parents — but she couldn't imagine that her part would change much. The
cool thing was this spying part — maybe her
character, Julie, would spy on the band in
other episodes too, maybe she'd have a regular part even if she didn't have many lines.

● ● ●

The next day, Kate and Maria were lying
in the lawn chairs on Kate's patio, a bit list-
less from what had become a bit of a heat
wave. Even though they were in the shade,
Kate had her sunglasses on. She took a sip of

her pop — it wasn't champagne, but it would have to do.

"So, who got our parts?" asked Maria.

"Take a wild guess," Kate said, wryly. "The glamour twins, of course."

"We should have known better than to think we had a chance."

"But Natalie's in the cast, though," Kate told her. "They changed George to Georgie."

"And the boys?"

"John is Bryce — you would have been John's sister. And Zack . . . remember him, the kid with all the jokes?"

"Sure," Maria replied. "He got B.B.? I'm not surprised. Who did they get for me instead?"

"Brooke."

Maria snorted. "I'd have been better. At least I have the same colouring as John."

"I don't know why you didn't take it," said Kate, shaking her head. "We could have been doing this together."

"Miss art class for one dumb line?" asked Maria. "No way."

"It's two lines, actually. You should have seen Tawny and Aimee sucking up to the grownups. It was sickening."

"I bet," Maria agreed, taking a sip of her pop.

Kate went on to tell Maria about the read–through and what happened, and about her lines and how she remembered Maria's dying bug and how it helped her. But her friend seemed bored. Well, it probably was more interesting if you were there.

" . . . and on Thursday, I have to go and get my costume done or something," she concluded.

"Thursday? But that's art day," said Maria.

"So what? I'm going to be an actress. I'll be on TV," Kate replied.

"Maybe." Maria looked doubtful.

"What do you mean: maybe?" snapped Kate. "Denise *said* . . . before. You were there. They're going to do six shows, and the network said they'd be on."

"I hope you're right," said Maria. "But I heard that these things practically never pan out. Just don't get too disappointed if it doesn't work out."

Why was everybody always telling her not to get disappointed? If things didn't work out, she'd be disappointed for sure, but she wouldn't die or anything. "So how was art on Tuesday?" Kate said, changing the subject.

"Good," replied Maria, getting interested again. "We were doing drawings of straight line objects — we had to draw, like, a chair or something and remember about perspective from last week. Shaylene opened the supply cupboard and drew practically everything in it. She's really good."

"You're good too," Kate told her friend.

"Mm . . . " Maria was non–committal.

"I wish I was as good as you," said Kate, with a sigh.

● ● ●

But Kate didn't have much time to worry about art class. She and Brooke had their costume fittings at the same time. As soon as they arrived at the office, Holly introduced them to a really cute guy with dark hair in a ponytail, called Kirk, who took them in a van to another building about two blocks away. Kate thought they could easily have walked it, but at the same time, it felt very official and movie–starry — even if it was a van, not a limo.

The building they arrived at was very large, made of red brick. At the front, there was a parking lot, and what looked like offices. Above the door there was a sign that said *Shooting Gallery,* and a large white A. But Kirk drove the van alongside the building and through a set of gates. Kate could see other parts of the building, marked B, C, and D. It was in front of C that Kirk parked the van.

"Have you met Pamela yet?" he asked them.

They shook their heads.

"You'll like her — wait and see." Kirk held the door open for them. Even though she knew that she could open her own door perfectly well, she felt very special and grown up to have someone like him hold a door for her. None of the boys in school ever did anything like that.

Kirk led the way through a maze of corridors and then through a door.

"Here they are, Pamela," said Kirk. "It's Kate and . . . Brooke? Right?"

"Ah, my latest victims," smiled Pamela. "Come into my parlour, girls."

Pamela was tall and big and very elegant, with a distinctly Caribbean accent. Her hair was piled on her head in a mass of tiny braids, and she was wearing a pair of loose pants printed in amber, ivory, and black, and a loose tunic top in ivory with a necklace made of enormous, irregular chunks of amber. Around her neck was a tape measure, and on her wrist she had a pincushion that Kate thought looked like a porcupine perched on her arm. She wore a pair of black–rimmed glasses and showed a wide, gap–toothed smile. Kate liked her right away.

"Now, honey, let's have a look at you," Pamela was saying to Brooke. "You're Brooke, are you? You're the little sister . . . what's her name, River? Oh, that's *very* good — Brooke, River. Oh yes . . . this is my assistant, Khadija"

A pretty, shy–looking, young woman smiled briefly at them. Kate was surprised to notice she was wearing Muslim headgear, and then wondered why she should have been surprised.

"I'll be back in an hour," said Kirk, and he was gone.

Kate sat down in a chair that was offered, and looked around the room while Pamela went to a clothes rack and began holding things up to Brooke. The room was a mess, for a start. Besides the clothing rack that Pamela was at, there were four others scattered around the room. On the floor were boxes of things like hats, skateboards, balls, and other toys. There were two or three bolts of fabric leaning in a corner and one partially unrolled on a table. A large mirror that had lost its silvering in one corner was leaning against a wall near an orange fabric divider that blocked off one corner. At the other end of the room were a sewing machine and ironing board. Fluorescent lights hung at the level where the ceiling should have been, but the ceiling itself was, Kate guessed, about two storeys higher.

Brooke was trying on various clothes including a really cute blue, green, and white outfit that Kate thought Maria would have looked great in, and Khadija was taking

Polaroid pictures of her in each costume.

Soon it was Kate's turn, but the outfits for her were almost all the same. First it was blue shorts with a green T–shirt, then purple shorts with a red T–shirt, then pink shorts with a white T– shirt, then green shorts with a green and white striped T–shirt. Kate liked the purple and red best, but she guessed from the look on Pamela's face that it wasn't her favourite. Khadija snapped her picture in each one — Kate was going blind with all the flashing.

Kate was no sooner back into her own clothes than Kirk arrived. She couldn't believe they'd really been there an hour. Brooke and Kate piled back into the van, and Kirk drove them the two blocks or so back to the office. Holly was waiting for them when they went back into the office.

"How'd it go?" she asked.

"Fine," said Kate and Brooke together. Kate wondered vaguely how it could have gone not fine.

"Good." Holly consulted a big binder with sheets all marked up with different colours of highlighter. "Rehearsal's at the Shooting Gallery, Monday at nine. It'll be all morning and probably run a little into the afternoon. We'll supply lunch if it does."

Kate felt nervous, but she could hardly wait.

SEVEN

Monday morning felt a long time in coming, but finally Kate pushed open the door to the Shooting Gallery and wondered where in the maze of corridors she was supposed to go. She needn't have worried — a big blue arrow pointed the direction. But anyway she could hear the sound of chatter not far away.

She went along the corridor, past the room where she had tried on the clothes, and turned right. At the end of that corridor, she found herself in a room even bigger than the school gym. Her breath caught in her throat. She was standing in a real movie studio.

The space was huge; the ceiling was the same one she had seen in the costume room. From where she was now, she could see that the offices had been built right into one part of the studio. A metal grid was suspended from the ceiling with huge lights hanging from it. Several tall step–ladders were scattered here and there, tall enough for the crew to climb and reach the lights, probably so they could adjust them, Kate guessed. People were standing in groups, talking, pointing occasionally, nodding. All the kids were together in one group, and Kate went over to join them.

"Isn't this cool, guys?" she said, as she came up to them. "Imagine, being in a *real* studio!"

Natalie grinned. "I know," she said, excitedly. Tawny and Aimee just gave her a look as if they'd been in and out of studios all their lives, though Kate knew that they hadn't.

"All right, people, listen up!" It was Denise, today in jeans and an oversized red T–shirt, but still with the tiger–eye pendant. As she touched the pendant briefly, Kate noticed that Denise's nails, while still short, didn't look quite as chewed.

Denise introduced the members of the crew that the kids had not already met and then explained what was to happen that day.

"We are going to go through the script scene by scene and work out exactly how it will be filmed. It will take a long time, so please be patient. When you are not in a scene, I'd appreciate it if you'd go to the green room, so that we're not distracted. There's juice and muffins there, and coffee and stuff, help yourselves. We'll start with scene one . . . "

Kate was not in scene one, so Kirk took her and the others who weren't needed to the green room. Kate was surprised that it was actually white, not green. There were a couple of old couches and armchairs, plus a table with wooden chairs. On shelves, some dog-eared books were piled neatly, as well as games of Clue, Trivial Pursuit, and a couple of others. Along one wall was a sink, microwave, coffee maker, a tray of juices, and a tray of muffins. But nothing was green.

Kate grabbed a banana muffin, and bounced down next to Natalie on a sofa. "Why do you suppose they call it the green room if it's not green?"

"Beats me," Natalie replied. "Hey, anybody know?"

"Know what?" asked Zack

"Why they call it the green room."

"It's from theatre," Tawny said, pronouncing the T properly, like the first one in pretentious. "All theatres" (that T again) "have a place for the actors to wait for their turn to go on. It's always called the green room."

"Why?" asked Kate, matter-of-factly.

"Nobody really knows. Some people think the original may have been green, and the name just stuck."

"Maybe the actors were turning green with nerves before they had to go on," Zack chimed in.

Kate laughed. "I like that explanation better," she said.

Tawny just looked at her. Oh brother, Kate thought, now she's going to hate me because I liked Zack's joke.

They all went on chatting for awhile. Soon Brooke came back and sent Tawny and Aimee to the studio, which for Kate anyway was a bit of a relief. It wasn't long before she was called on set.

Somebody gave her a newspaper bag, with a few newspapers in it. Denise explained.

"We're actually going to film this scene outside," she told Kate. "You'll be walking on a sidewalk, crossing the scene from left to right — that's my left — deliver the paper, deliver your line and that's it. Want to try it?"

Kate went to the place she was told to begin, and when Denise nodded, she walked across.

"Here's your paper, Mr. Simpson," she called. Good. This time she remembered the dying bug *before* she said the line. But she couldn't get the paper out — it got caught in the bag.

One or two more walk–throughs and everything seemed to be fine. Zack, John, Tawny, Aimee, and Natalie all came on set then. Denise and all the others moved to a garage that had been built inside the studio for filming in.

"Let's get the front off, guys," called Denise, and immediately a couple of men, (they were called grips, Kate had learned) appeared with power screwdrivers. Eight quick zips and the whole front of the garage was off. Inside, it looked just like a garage should look. A workbench had tools hanging on a pegboard. A bicycle was leaning in one corner. Cans of paint stood on shelves. And in the middle were instruments — two electric guitars, regular and bass, a drum kit, and a keyboard.

The main characters must have had an earlier rehearsal, because they all went straight over and picked up or positioned themselves behind instruments. It looked just like a rerun of — what was that old show they were always rerunning with the family in a bus? *The Partridge Family!* From the workbench Tawny picked up a tambourine that Kate had not noticed before.

"All right, Kate," said Denise, "the front of the garage will be on, with the door open when we film the first part of this scene. You are going by, and you see everyone inside the garage. You go up to them . . . that's right . . . go inside the garage — and the rest of the scene will be filmed with the front off."

They worked through the scene. Considering it was only ten lines long (there were a few more lines from the band members after "Julie" left the scene), it took ages to "block," as Denise called it. Kate had thought that they would just go through the actions, like in a play. But the camera would be shooting from several different angles — the shots would be pieced together later. The actions that worked from one angle didn't work from another, and Denise and Colin, the cinematographer (that's cameraman — or woman — to anyone other than Colin), kept changing what they wanted everyone to do.

In the breaks between looking at the different angles, Aimee kept saying things like, "I'm ready for my close–up, Mr. DeMille," and fluffing her hair, which Kate found idiotic. For one thing, she didn't think there was anyone there *called* Mr. DeMille, but other people seemed to think it was funny. Finally, the scene was blocked, and it was time for lunch. Which was a good thing, because Kate was exhausted.

Lunch was pretty good. Everyone got their own cardboard box marked *Reel Meals*, and inside was a sandwich, a little salad in a clear plastic dish with a lid, a can of pop, a butter tart, an apple or banana, and a red and white checkered paper napkin.

The afternoon scenes were not as tiring for Kate, because she was only in three and had no lines. In one, she just had to stand on the driveway until the band closed the garage door. In another, she was outside the garage trying to peer into a window that was too high, and in the third she had found a pail to stand on. This one was going to be shot from inside and outside the garage.

• • •

Luckily there was no rehearsal on Tuesday, so Kate was able to go to art class again with Maria. She was dying to tell her all about everything on set. Maria was waiting on her porch steps when Kate arrived, and they each gave a camel wave as Maria got up and they started down the sidewalk.

"Maria, you really should have taken that part. Even though it was only two lines, it was so interesting . . . "

"Stop saying I should have taken the part. I didn't, okay?" snapped Maria.

"Sor–ree!" said Kate and then instantly regretted snapping. To cover her embarassment, she rushed on. "The room was just huge! And I said all my lines right — I thought of you doing the 'dying bug' — and I'm in three other scenes too, even though I don't say anything. And I might get a close–up! They have a green room and it's not even green, and they shoot everything from about seventeen thousand different directions — angles, I mean — and the lunch came in a box, the company was called *Reel Meals*, r–e–e–l, get it? Can you believe there's a company that especially makes lunches for filming? 'Cause I mean, they must, or why else would they call themselves that?"

"They must, I guess," said Maria listlessly.

Kate knew she shouldn't go on, because obviously . . . well, actually, she wasn't sure what it was with Maria. Maybe she was regretting turning down the part, or maybe she was a little jealous because the part Kate had been offered was four lines, while the sister part was only two. But she had to tell her about Aimee, and the garage.

"And Aimee kept acting stupid and saying, 'I'm ready for my close–up, Mr. DeMille,' whatever that was all about."

"It's a line from an old movie," Maria said. "Trust Aimee."

"I know," said Kate, rolling her eyes. "Also, the garage the band plays in . . . the whole front comes off, so they can light it, Denise said, and they can kind of look around it more with the camera . . . what old movie?"

"*Sunset Boulevard*," Maria said. "You remember, we saw it on TV when you slept over."

"We did?"

"Just in the spring. When we were finishing up the cow project."

"About the old movie star? I don't

80

remember that line."

"No, I think you were still messing around with the project, writing out the cards or something, now that I think about it. Anyway, the garage sounds cool," said Maria, and now she did sound as if she wanted to know more. Well, enough about filming.

"What have I missed at art?"

"We've just been working on the object drawings some more. Pick something easy, and you'll catch up soon. Like a book, or something."

They arrived at the school where the art class was held, and went down to the classroom. Maria went straight to sit with Shaylene, and Kate joined her at the same table. A few other girls arrived and joined them — Kate knew two of them were Lauras, whom Maria referred to as "long–hair Laura" and "short–hair Laura." When long–hair Laura got there and saw Kate, she said, "Oh, Kate's here," and brought a chair over from another table. Kate sort of felt like she didn't belong or something, but she didn't want to move. She only really knew Maria — and Shaylene, sort of. The other table had mostly boys and two girls that Kate didn't know at all. So she watched silently as they got their partly finished artwork out of the cupboard and set up their pencils and their pens and ink.

"Hey, that's my ink," protested short–hair Laura when Shaylene picked up a bottle.

"Steal–o–RAM–a!" said Shaylene, in a funny voice. They all cracked up.

Kate looked at Maria, puzzled. Obviously she knew what was going on, because she was laughing, too. Maria caught her look.

"Sorry," she said between gulps of laughter. "In joke . . . too complicated . . . you had to be there."

Kate smiled, to show she was willing to go along with whatever it was, that she'd catch up. After all, she had missed two classes.

"Hey, guys, we have to go to another movie this weekend," said long–hair Laura.

Another movie?

"You went to the movies?" asked Kate.

"Yeah," Shaylene said. "Steal–o–RAM–a!" Everybody started laughing again. "We saw *The Sheriff of Apple Pie County*. Didn't Maria tell you?"

Kate looked at Maria.

"Oh, you were too busy with your TV show," Maria said casually. "Laura, can you pass me that eraser, please?"

"Not on the weekend, I wasn't," said Kate, quietly. She must have said it too quietly, she guessed, because Maria didn't seem to hear her.

82

EIGHT

After class, Maria and Kate walked home slowly together. The heat wave hadn't let up, but the big maple trees threw a shady canopy over the street.

"I kind of wish you'd called me about the movie," Kate said. "I could have gone — I wasn't doing anything."

"I know . . . I'm honestly sorry," Maria replied. "I never really thought about it. Shaylene just called me, so I said okay. Next time I'll call you, though."

Kate smiled. So it was all right, she hadn't deliberately been left out, not by Maria anyway. She still felt a little bit neglected because she'd been forgotten, but after all she'd missed a couple of classes, and she didn't know Shaylene very well.

● ● ●

Once filming began, Kate didn't have much time to worry about going to the movies. Filming turned out to be even more painstaking than rehearsal — which made sense, since it was the finished product after all.

The first day was very exciting. As soon as she arrived, Kate could tell everything was different, bigger, more important. Holly was at the main entrance with a clipboard, and she directed Kate to a room across the hall from the green room. Brooke and the lady playing Zack's mother were already there. Pamela greeted her as she came in.

"There you are, hon. Come on, please change into these."

It was the green and blue shorts set. Not too bad. When she was dressed, Kate was sent to the green room to wait.

Natalie was in the green room too, and they got a game of checkers going after a while. As before, there was juice and muffins, and also fruit, cereal and milk, bagels, bread and a toaster, and jam, peanut butter, and butter. Kate chose an apple.

"I wonder why we had to come so early, if they don't need us." Kate chomped a huge bite out of the apple.

"Maybe they didn't know it would take so long," said Natalie.

The checkers game was done, and still they hadn't been called. Everyone else was on set, so they were alone. Natalie was braiding her long black hair into thin strips which, because her hair was so straight, came undone almost immediately. Kate watched the pulsating dot on the microwave that marked the seconds.

"I'm taking tap–dancing lessons," Natalie announced suddenly.

"Oh, yeah? Teach me something," said Kate, glad for something to do.

"They don't start until next week," said Natalie.

"Oh." The girls fell silent again.

Finally they were called.

Kate couldn't believe the difference in the studio. First of all, besides the cast, there were about thirty people in the room. But the main thing was that the cavernous emptiness was gone. The garage was still set up on one side, but now it was surrounded by lights, ladders, wooden boxes, some heavy–looking bags, cables, people, chairs, and all kinds of other equipment. Another set had been built in the previously empty space, which was meant to be someone's kitchen. Some chairs were facing the garage — they were actual folding, canvas, "director's" chairs! Kate had just sort of assumed that was a cliché, and they wouldn't really have such things, but there they were. They didn't have people's names on them though. Along the wall behind the chairs was a table set up with all the same food they had in the green room, plus doughnuts. Kate wondered who would ever eat all this stuff, but she noticed some of the guys were pretty brawny, so maybe they needed it.

To Kate's surprise, they shot the scene where Julie asks to join the band first, not the "Here's your paper" scene. The front of the garage was on, and the door was open.

Denise asked the cast to walk through the scene one more time, just as a last rehearsal before filming. "Places, everyone!" she called out authoritatively. Kate noticed that although she still wore the pendant, Denise wasn't fiddling with it today. Kate wondered about this, and then figured it out. Denise was in her element; she was directing, and she was focussed only on that — she didn't need her soothing stone right now.

On cue, Kate walked forward into the garage.

"Okay, hold it," said Denise. "Give her a sandbag."

Kirk ran into the scene, carrying one of the heavy-looking bags, and set it at Kate's left toe. "Stop walking when you feel that," he explained to her quietly, "and don't look down — do it by feel. That way you end up in the exact spot they want you."

"Let's get the line, now," called Denise.

"You guys are starting a band?" asked Kate.

"Good, go on." They continued the scene.

"Okay, we'll go with the master first," said Denise. Kate knew a lot of this had been explained to them in the training, but she couldn't remember half of it and had only the vaguest idea of what was going on. All she knew was that they had to do the scene over and over and over, not because people were getting their lines wrong, necessarily — although that happened too — but for all kinds of reasons that Kate could barely detect.

"I'm getting a shadow," Colin would say, or, "I'm catching glare off the window," and Kirk or someone would run over and adjust a light or spray something on the window. Even Kate's glasses needed a spray of something to keep them from glinting.

And it wasn't just the camera. The guy who recorded the sound called a halt once, and, of course, Denise would stop them or make them do it over if she didn't like the way something looked or sounded. And on top of all that, once they had the scene the way Denise wanted it, they had to film from a couple of other angles, though Kate was not sure why. Finally, the scene was done, and everyone took a break for lunch.

Even though she was glad of the break, Kate was sorry her big scene was done. The whole scene would cover maybe a minute or less on TV, but it had taken nearly a whole morning to film. The endless, tiny adjustments being made, a guy with a goatee taking pictures of the scene with a couple of fancy–looking cameras slung around his neck, and somebody else called Jen jumping in between takes to snap Polaroid pictures, which she then labeled, hole–punched and kept on a big ring on her belt.

Kate had intended to ask Jen at lunchtime what she was doing, but the crew members all ate at one table, while the cast sat at another. Denise came and sat at the cast table for a little while and drank a cup of coffee.

"How are you all holding up?" she asked the group of kids.

"Great," said Kate right away.

"My feet are sore," complained Aimee.

"Well, raise them up during lunch, and you'll be fine for the afternoon." Denise moved on to chat with the crew and soon went into her own office.

"There's chocolate brownies," Kate observed. "Anyone want one?"

"Yes, please!" Natalie spoke up.

"Could you get me an apple?" asked Aimee, in the same petulant voice, as if her feet wouldn't bear walking on.

"Sure," said Kate and went over to the

table where the desserts were. She chose two big brownies and a nice–looking red apple and carried them back on a plate. When she had set the plate down on the table, she realized that Aimee had her feet up on what had been Kate's chair. Kate looked at her.

"You heard Denise," said Aimee, defensively. "I have to put my feet up. You can find another chair."

"As far away from you as possible," retorted Kate, and she picked up her brownie and went to the crew table.

"Thanks for the brownie," called Natalie, as Kate walked away.

Kate felt a little funny going to a table full of grown–ups she barely knew, but she wasn't going to wait around and be treated like a slave for Aimee. The seat next to Jen was open, so she sat down there.

"Hi, Kate," said Jen, sounding a little surprised.

"Hi, Jen . . . um . . . I was wondering what all the polaroids are for . . . that's all."

Jen smiled. "Oh . . . well, my job is continuity, so I have to keep a record of costumes, props, and stuff. If we need to reshoot something, or if they add another scene that takes place on the same day, we can get the actors into the identical clothes. You've heard of all those famous movie bloopers where someone will be wearing, say, a necklace, and then it's gone — and then it magically reappears?"

Kate nodded.

"Well, it's my job to make sure that does-n't happen."

"Cool," said Kate. "It sounds hard. You must have a good memory."

"That's important, but the polaroids help. At the end of the day, I stick them in a big photo album scene by scene."

"But what about the other guy, the one with the fancy cameras. Don't his pictures show that stuff? Why do it twice?"

"Oh, you mean Paul," said Jen. "No, his pictures are for publicity — totally different from what I'm doing."

"Oh," said Kate. More and more stuff! More and more people! She was never going to understand it all. Before she could ask more questions, though, everyone was called back from lunch, and the actors sent to the green room to wait for their next call.

"Well, here's Miss Goody-Two-Shoes sucking up to the crew," said Aimee, in a snarky voice when Kate arrived in the room.

"Well, at least I keep my shoes on the *floor*," Kate muttered to Natalie, probably just a little too loudly. It wasn't the greatest comeback, but it was the best she could come up with on the spot.

• • •

Kate was exhausted when she got home from the set each evening. So much sitting around, followed by so much concentrating: remembering each line and the actions to go with it, walking where she was supposed to, feeling the sandbag for her place to stop, but not looking down, conveying the feeling of being let down when she walked away from the garage. But she was happy.

At dinner, she would babble about her day, what she had done and seen and learned. She chatted excitedly about the polaroid pictures, the green room, and the canvas chairs. Both her parents seemed interested in all the intricacies, and it was fun to know about something they didn't. It was especially fun the day Kate filmed the scene with her line, "Here's your paper, Mr. Simpson," because it was so different from the days she was in the studio.

The first difference was that they were outside, at a house with a real garage that looked exactly like the one in the studio. The other big difference was that there was hardly anyone there. Kate was the only actor — there wasn't even a "Mr. Simpson," since, as Kirk explained, he wouldn't show anyway — and there seemed to be fewer crew members than before. Kate was sent into a Winnebago to change into her costume, the blue and green shorts set, and the newspaper bag.

Then she was told to check in with Jen.

Jen looked her over and showed her the photo album where she had filed the polaroids from the first day of shooting.

"Your newspaper bag was over the other shoulder," she pointed out, and Kate switched it. Now that she understood that things were filmed in many ways and pieced together later, she realized why it was important to have a person for continuity. It certainly would have looked strange if she had walked up to the garage with the bag on one shoulder — and then have it magically jump to the other side once she was in the garage.

• • •

All too soon, the filming of her episode was finished, and Kate was dumped back into regular life. She hadn't seen Maria for a whole week, and she'd missed two art classes, so she was feeling a bit nervous when she went to call for her on Thursday to go to class.

Maria looked surprised when she answered the door to Kate.

"Hi . . . don't you have to film today?" she asked.

"No, the episode is done. I'm back again."

"Yay!" replied Maria.

As they walked along together, Maria

updated her on all the art class gossip. It didn't make much sense to Kate, because she didn't know all the people Maria was talking about, but she figured she'd catch up eventually. Kate didn't say too much about filming since Maria didn't seem to care much about what had happened on set. But then again, why would she?

The rest of the crowd were friendly to her in class and helped her out because she was horribly behind. Afterwards, the whole gang went for popsicles, which were just right for the hot, muggy August day. It hadn't rained for ages, and nobody was supposed to be using their sprinklers. Still, a few people had them on anyway, and as Maria and Kate wandered home they walked through any that were going, just for that wonderful burst of cold water, and then the brief feeling of coolness as they dried off.

Kate knew that the read–through for the next episode was on Friday, and though no one had said anything, she kind of hoped there would be another part for Julie. But it was Thursday already, and she hadn't heard anything. Surely there would be a message on the machine when she got home. But the little red light wasn't blinking. She checked to make sure the machine was on, and it was. Oh well, maybe Julie would just be spying in the background again. No reason to bring

Kate into a read–through if she didn't have any actual lines.

Dinner was spanakopita that her dad had picked up on his way home from work. It was usually one of Kate's favourites, but somehow she didn't feel very hungry in the heat, and she mostly cut pieces and moved them around her plate. She ate a little, and it tasted okay, but she just didn't want very much.

Kate's mom noticed.

"What is it, honey? Something wrong?"

"No . . . just tired, I guess."

"It's too hot, isn't it?" commented her mom.

"The acting's wearing you out," suggested her dad.

"Well, it's not going to do that any more," sighed Kate.

"You don't know that for sure," encouraged her mom.

"Don't you think they would have called by now, if they wanted me tomorrow for the read–through?"

"Maybe they'll need you for the next episode," soothed her mom.

"Don't, Carla. You'll raise her hopes . . . maybe for nothing," said her dad.

"Bill . . . please," said her mother, in a tired voice. "Don't be unkind."

Dad took a sip of his wine. The glass was drenched in condensation. "I'm trying to be kind. Raise her hopes, and she could be disappointed. Don't expect things, and if they work out it's a nice surprise."

"I have to get caught up on my art project," Kate announced, pushing her chair out from the table, and pushed back a lock of hair, frizzed in the humidity. As she climbed the stairs, she could hear her parents' argument wind on.

"You're putting wild, romantic notions into the child's head."

"She's doing what *she* wants to . . . "

Kate closed the door on the voices. She could still hear them, but they were far away, as though they were in somebody else's life. "And what *do* I want to do?" she murmured to herself. It made her think of the line in *A Chorus Line*: "Who am I anyway?" Was she her daddy's little girl? Her mother's smart and beautiful Kate? Well, she wasn't beautiful, not with that wild hair. She wasn't smart, not very smart. She had to work pretty hard in school to get those As and Bs. And she certainly wasn't little. Not so very big either, but she was starting high school this fall. Kate had always believed that somewhere in her very middle was an off–white, wiggly piece of gristle that was her core, her true self, her soul maybe. What was that core made of? What was her true self?

Kate lay down on her striped bedspread

and stared at the ceiling. Life used to be so simple. School, hanging out with Maria, helping her mom with stuff, dinner in the kitchen. But now she had an ambition, to be an actress, and it wasn't working out the way she dreamed. And her dad — who always used to call her "princess" and "pal" and used to take her to the ballet and to the movies — seemed to be someone else, seemed so far away these days. But then again, she didn't really need him to take her to the movies, since she went with her friends now. Was that it? Was she pushing him away? Was he angry with her for growing up? But she had to, it was the way things were, she *was* more grown up now, and she needed to start being herself. Funny, she thought, that acting was what she wanted to do — to be herself by being someone else. And yet, to Kate, it made perfect sense.

Downstairs, it seemed her parents had stopped arguing. She couldn't hear their voices any more anyway. Sure enough, a few moments later, she heard her dad's footsteps coming up the stair, passing her door, and going into the study. From two rooms away, Kate could hear Beethoven playing softly on the CD player.

Since it really was way too early for bed, Kate rolled over and picked up the phone beside her bed. It was times like these that it was so fabulous to have someone like Maria for a friend.

It was Maria who answered the phone.

"Hi, it's me," said Kate. "Doing anything?"

"Just watching TV, babysitting Tonio, sweating."

"Can I come over?"

"Sure," said Maria. "Trouble on the home front?"

"Just my parents, squabbling again."

"Come on over," said Maria. "I'll make popcorn."

When Kate arrived at Maria's, she found Maria in the kitchen, which was filled with the inviting aroma of popcorn. The girls carried their popcorn and pop into the living room, where Tonio was standing up in his playpen.

"Oh, look how big you're getting," Kate burbled to him and tapped his tiny nose.

"Gak!" said Tonio and broke into a grin, just before he lost his balance and bounced down onto his behind.

"I think that's why they put diapers on kids," said Maria. "Extra padding."

As the sky turned to fire, the shrieks of the neighbourhood kids playing hide–and–seek drifted in. "Ready or not, here I come!"

"So, what's up?" Maria started.

"Well . . . " Now Kate wondered whether she should have come over to talk to Maria, since it all started with talking about *Backbeat*. But she was here now — might as well get on with it. "I know you're not as interested in the acting thing as I am, but I really wanted to get a part on the show. Anyway, I didn't get called for episode two, and I mentioned that I was disappointed. The next thing you know, my parents are in a fight."

"Sorry . . . I must have missed something there," Maria stopped her. "How did that get them into a fight?"

"It was about whether or not I should get my hopes up."

"Why should *they* fight about that? It's *your* hopes."

"I know, that's what's so weird," Kate agreed. "I was thinking in my room about how great my dad and I used to get along, and now it seems like he's mad at me all the time."

"Are you doing anything to make him mad?"

"No!" said Kate, with frustration. "That's what I can't figure out. The only thing I can see that I'm doing is growing up. Maybe he doesn't like it."

"Like he can stop it," laughed Maria.

"It's just, like, with the show and every-thing, I felt real . . . I felt like I was starting to be someone I wanted to be. I don't mean Julie . . . I don't mean the character . . . I'm not sure what I mean. I just know . . . you know?"

Maria nodded as she teased Tonio with a toy.

Kate went on. "It's like my dad wants me to be . . . well, I don't know what he wants me to be. But I want him to see what me *is*."

"Me is?" asked Maria, with laughter in her voice.

"Yeah." Kate put on a deep voice. "Me is Kate. You Tarzan. Ooh! ooh!" She beat her chest.

Tonio clapped and squawked happily. Outside, someone called, "Home–free!"

"Aw, I guess it's just bad tempers," Kate said, shaking her head. "Everyone's too hot."

NINE

Kate had clung to a faint hope that she might be in episode two, even without lines. But the phone remained silent, though both it and the answering machine seemed to be working fine otherwise. Art class went on. There were only a couple of weeks of classes left, the weather remained hot, though more bearable, and the girls often went for popsicles afterward. They were always friendly, and Kate got along fine with them. But she had missed so many classes that she never quite felt part of the gang.

Then, one day, the phone did ring.

Assuming it was Maria, Kate idly picked up the receiver.

"Hullo?"

"Hello, this is Johnson Cormier calling for Kate," came Mr. Cormier's formal–sounding voice down the line.

Kate sat bolt upright. Mr. Cormier seemed nice, but he made her a little nervous. He was always wearing a suit and seemed a little distracted, as if he was thinking about networks and words from our sponsor all the time.

"Hello, Mr. Cormier . . . it's me," said Kate. Oh no, should that have been, "It's I"? But no one in their right mind would say, "It's I," would they? But Mr. Cormier didn't seem to mind. Or maybe he didn't notice.

"Kate, as we said at the time, we were very pleased with your audition, and I'm sure Denise told you what a good job you did on episode one."

Denise hadn't, not specifically, but it was nice to hear now.

Mr. Cormier went on. "We've been in discussions with our writers, and it's been decided to expand the role of Julie . . . "

Kate squeaked. She couldn't help it.

"Sorry?"

"Nothing, Mr. Cormier. You were saying?"

"Yes, well . . . you would need to talk it over with your parents first, and then Denise and I would talk to them. It would most likely mean missing some school in the fall."

"Can't I say yes already?" pleaded Kate.

"Well, I'm glad you want to do it, Kate. But it's very important that your parents understand the implications and that they agree to allow you. Perhaps you could discuss it this evening and have them call me tomorrow?"

"Okay, Mr. Cormier. Thank you. Thank you *so much!*"

As soon as Kate hung up the phone, she went bounding around the living room, bouncing on the sofa and whooping at the top of her lungs. Julie was back! Julie was back!

As soon as she had that out of her system, she bounced back to the chair and dialled Maria's number. Luisa answered.

"No, sorry, Kate, Maria's out with the girls. They went to a matinee. She'll be back soon, I'll tell her to call you."

"Okay." Kate set the receiver back in its cradle.

Kate grabbed her Tetris Gameboy and went out to sit on the porch chair. Then, what Luisa had said struck her. What did she mean — Maria's out with "the girls"? What girls? Why would Maria go out without her? In spite of the exciting news from Mr. Cormier, she was starting to feel crabby. She was crabby about Maria, and she was crabby she had no one to tell her good news to, and she was crabby because, in spite of her willingness to say yes to Mr. Cormier right away, she wasn't at all sure that her parents would agree. She clicked the little buttons furiously, trying to get the little shapes to fall into place.

Accidentally dropping an L–shaped piece into the wrong place, Kate quit the game and started a new one. Just then, she heard voices coming up the street. Glancing up, she saw it was Maria and "the girls" — short and long hair Lauras, Shaylene, and the others from art class. She concentrated deeply on the game, waiting to glance up only when they were right in front of her house.

She paused the game and looked up, with a smile. She wasn't going to let them know she knew anything or felt anything.

"Hi, guys," she called out, with a brittle cheerfulness.

"Hi, Kate," said Shaylene and short–hair Laura, together. The other Laura waved.

Slowly Maria turned toward the front porch where Kate was sitting, as if she hadn't seen her yet, or maybe didn't know Kate lived there. "Oh, hi," she said casually, and walked on. About half a house away, she said something to the others, and everyone laughed as they moved out of earshot. Kate unpaused the game, and let the little squares fall wherever they landed.

A few minutes later, the phone rang.

Kate went into the house and picked it up, gingerly.

"Hello?"

"Hi, Kate, it's me. Luisa said you called."

"Yeah, I did," said Kate and stopped.

"Well? What's up?"

"Nothing important. I have to go set the table. Talk to you later."

"Oh . . . okay." Maria sounded a little surprised, maybe a little put out. Well, good.

"Bye," said Kate and put down the phone.

Kate's mind felt like a swamp as she set out the forks and knives for dinner. It was like one of those swamps that looks like you could walk across it, but . . . no, Kate knew exactly what it was like: it was like in the cartoons when people jumped onto logs and they turned out to be crocodiles. Think about the first phone call, she told herself. Mr. Cormier and Denise thought you were good — they've expanded your role *because you're good*, she told herself. Think about how you're going to talk your parents into this. Forget about Maria: she's just an old crocodile, she told herself. Maria went to the movies without you, and she didn't even care, she heard herself say back.

Concentrate! Mom and Dad will be home any minute, and you've got to prepare your argument, just like Dad does for court. Because this was sure no automatic yes.

• • •

Kate decided to wait until dinner to tell her parents about the expanded part. To help smooth the way, she made a salad. Usually, her mom did the cooking. She always said she found it a nice way to put a space between work and home, so Kate didn't prepare anything else. For her dad, she set out a glass, his Scotch, and a bowl of ice. Finally, she went to the garden and snipped a rose, which she put into a small vase in the centre of the table.

It wasn't long before Kate's mom and dad came in through the front door. Since they usually drove to work together, they usually came home together too.

"Well, this is service," said her dad, pleased when he saw the Scotch and ice laid out.

"Oh my . . . and a salad made too!" exclaimed her mom when she went into the kitchen. "What are you up to, Kate? It's not even report card time."

Kate just smiled. "I felt restless . . . I wanted something to do," she answered.

Soon, they were all sitting around the dinner table, with steaming bowls of pasta bolognese in front of them, wine poured for the adults, and milk for Kate. Kate helped herself to a plate of salad.

"So, anyway . . . I got a call from Mr. Cormier today," Kate said, casually. "Julie's going to be in the next episode."

"That's fabulous, honey," said her mom enthusiastically.

"Good for you," said her dad.

Whew! Made the first hurdle. "He said they might need her for some more episodes too," Kate went on, starting to smile, in spite of herself.

"More episodes?" Her dad's tone changed. "Isn't it getting awfully close to school starting?"

Oh–oh. "Ye–es," said Kate. "He said it was *possible* I might miss a little bit of school. He wants you to call tomorrow, just to say it's okay."

"I take it, then, that means you will definitely miss a fair bit of school," her father said casually. Kate felt cautious. This felt like some cross–examination trick. What exactly *had* Mr. Cormier said?

"Bill . . . " Kate's mother started, but Kate interrupted. This was one battle she needed to win — or lose — by herself.

"I'm telling you what he said! He said I might miss a bit of school. He didn't say a lot." Kate realized she was nearly shouting.

Her dad looked at Kate for a moment or two, then down at his pasta. He took a bite, chewed it thoughtfully, and swallowed it with a sip of wine. "I don't think I like the idea of you missing school," he finally said.

Kate was trembling inside, but she knew she had to fight for this. She couldn't get emotional, not if she was arguing with a lawyer. Keep calm now, Kate, keep in control. State your case. You *know* what you want. This is how to get it. Kate set down her fork, and smoothed the edge of her place mat. She took a deep breath, and then she spoke.

"Dad . . . I am a very good student in school. You know it. My last report card was all As and Bs, and sure . . . I could do better in geography and gym, but I probably won't. Acting is something *I* want to do. It might not be my career, but *I* want to do it. To do it, I know I will have to keep my marks up, and I will do whatever it takes to make that happen, if it means I can keep acting."

Kate stopped abruptly. Well, that probably tore it. She'd never spoken to her parents in such a tone of voice — they'd probably be furious with her. Even her mom wouldn't be on her side now. Kate picked up her fork and took a mouthful of pasta. She couldn't chew it, and it hurt going down. She kept her gaze on the plate as the silence grew. Finally her father stood up, and picked up his wine glass.

"I'll be in the study," he said, reaching for the bottle of wine. But he paused and seemed to think the better of it, and went upstairs leaving the bottle on the table.

Kate looked at her mom, who had been quiet all this time. She was looking oddly at Kate. "Don't worry, honey, I think he might come around. Don't get your hopes *too* high." Her mom paused and with a faraway look, she said again, "But I think he might come around."

Kate and her mom cleared the dishes away and put the dishwasher on, not talking much. Kate's mom seemed preoccupied, and Kate was totally distracted. Her mind didn't seem to know where to land. Would her father say yes or no? What was up with Maria? Ooh . . . don't think about that! Denise and Mr. Cormier thought she was good. She kept trying to hold on only to that thought, but another little voice trickled in: Yeah, but what good does that do you if Dad says no?

When the kitchen was cleaned up, her mom suggested they watch TV. Kate had nothing better to do, so she agreed.

It was nothing but sitcoms that Kate had mostly already seen, which was probably just as well, since she couldn't concentrate anyway. Guessing from her dad's reaction, Kate figured her cause was doomed. But her mom seemed to think there was reason for hope. Her mom was crocheting, and Kate found the repetitive rhythm soothing. She'd have to get her mom to show her how someday. Kate turned sideways in the armchair, dangling her legs over the arm. Gradually, she swung around, so that she was lying on the seat of the chair, with her legs over the back. Classical music was drifting faintly down the stairs.

"You're not worrying about your dad, are

you?" asked Kate's mother. "You know when he plays Mozart, it'll be all right. It's Beethoven you want to worry about."

"Really?" asked Kate. "I never knew that. I like Beethoven. I like *Für Elise* and *The Moonlight Sonata.*"

"They're for blue moods," explained her mom. "Mozart is for sorting things out."

"That's weird. Why?"

"Well, if you listen, Beethoven is all romantic and mysterious and mushy. There's a cleanness to the sound of Mozart — it's busy, but everything's in the right place. Your dad likes things . . . orderly. That's why he's such a good lawyer — law makes sense to him."

"Well, *that* makes sense to me," agreed Kate.

"That was quite the speech you gave him tonight, hon. From the heart, but logical. He'll have liked that."

"You think so?" Kate could feel hope welling higher in her heart.

With that same faraway look on her face, Kate's mom dropped the rhythm of her crocheting for a moment. "You two are a lot alike."

This was an unexpected thought, and Kate mulled it over for a while. It was probably true. Though she liked new things, she liked to keep the old things, too. Like old friends. Like Maria.

Kate stretched her arm out and retrieved her Gameboy (why not Gamegirl, or Gamekid, she wondered idly) from where she'd left it on the coffee table. The music from upstairs stopped, and Kate heard footsteps on the stairs.

"So," said Kate's dad as he came into the living room, "I guess you must be excited about your part being expanded."

In an instant, Kate's spirits soared. "Oh, Dad . . . you mean it? I can do it? Oh thank you!" She leaped across the room and gave her dad a hug.

"Okay, princess. You just make sure you don't let those marks slip." His voice was serious, but he stroked her hair. "But I know you will. You're a smart girl."

TEN

Kate was filled with — well, joy — but mainly relief that her father had allowed her to continue with *Backbeat*. And maybe a little bit of pride. She had kept her head and presented her case, and maybe earned a little bit of new respect. But she still couldn't shake that gloominess, the stinging feeling of Maria not calling her to go to the movies.

"I'm afraid I've got to do a little work," said Kate's father, heading back upstairs. "I'll be in the study if anyone needs me."

Kate picked up her Gameboy and started a new game of Tetris.

"You're very quiet," commented Kate's mom.

"Just thinking about stuff, I guess," replied Kate.

"I thought you'd be excited about the part," Mom went on. "I thought you'd be over at Maria's hatching plans to take over Hollywood. What did she say when she found out?"

111

"She doesn't know. I thought I'd wait and make sure it was okay with you guys first."

Her mother gave her a skeptical look, and Kate swung around to face her. "Actually, she doesn't want to talk about *Backbeat* any more." Even Kate heard a surprising bitter tone in her own voice.

Her mom stopped crocheting. "Is she jealous, do you think?"

Kate shrugged. "She doesn't even know I'm getting more than four lines. I think she's just not interested."

Her mom's fingers took up their rhythmic turn–turn–hook, turn–turn–hook. Kate watched her complete a row.

"Not interested in me, I guess," Kate went on. "It's funny, we're — we *were* — best friends for so long, ever since *Peter Pan* and especially when we were working on the cow project, and winning the red ribbon, and now it's like . . . she's just got no time for me."

"Sometimes people change," replied her mom. "But more likely, there's a simple explanation. She's busy, or preoccupied, or something. It could be something at home."

"I'm probably not being fair, anyway. Like you said, there's probably an explanation. And sometimes she's friendly. I'm probably just misunderstanding." Kate yawned. "So you'll call Mr. Cormier tomorrow?"

"First thing," said her mom. "And you

know, you can't make anyone do anything but yourself. If Maria keeps acting unfriendly, all you can do is decide how you'll react. Will you let it drag you down, or will you rise above it?"

Kate nodded. "Right now, I think I'll go to bed," she said.

In bed, with the light off, Kate could hear the faint, somehow comforting clicking of the computer keyboard in her dad's study, and she knew that her mom's afghan was getting slowly bigger with each turn–turn–hook. Kate thought about that piece of gristle in the middle of her. Right now, in spite of what her mom said, she could feel it twisting, burning, glowing, like the wrong colour of sky. Sailor's warning. She closed her eyes. Turn–turn–hook. Click clicky click clicky click. The Tetris boxes falling and falling and landing neatly in their slots, the line cleared away, and pieces constantly falling, always more pieces falling into their places.

• • •

It was still pretty hot out the next day, and Kate was alone in the house. Somehow, she hesitated about calling Maria with the good news about her part being expanded. And that was just plain weird. Kate and Maria practically lived in each other's pockets, and Kate had never held back from talking to her about anything before. And this was *good* news. Finally, she decided to go to Maria's house and just see the lay of the land before she said anything.

Maria came to the door when Kate rang the bell — another thing that was odd, as the girls usually just rang and then went in, at least during the day. Kate thought Maria's expression changed when she saw her, as if she had been expecting someone else.

"Oh . . . hi," Maria greeted Kate without much enthusiasm.

Kate gave her usual "camel wave", and Maria looked blank, then waved back. "Come in," said Maria. "What's new?"

She had to tell her, she had to. With studied casualness, she said, "They're having 'Julie' on *Backbeat* again." She started to grin — she couldn't help it.

"Who's Julie?" asked Maria — and then quickly remembered. "Oh, yeah, your character. That's great."

"Yeah, I'm kind of excited." Kind of excited? That was the understatement of the year.

Just then the doorbell rang, and Maria turned to answer it. Shaylene stood on the other side of the screen, and she made a motion like an underhand "camel wave." Maria returned the gesture.

"Hi, Shaylene. I'm almost ready — come on in."

"Hi, Kate," said Shaylene when she saw her. Maria took off to her room and left the two standing there.

"Hi," Kate responded. "What's this?" Kate gave the underhand "camel wave."

"Oh, it's just a wave me and Maria do," said Shaylene. "It's a 'smile wave,' see?" She gave the wave again. "Maria thought of it — it's from our initials, S.S. and M.L . . . .smile — get it?"

"Oh," was all Kate said. But inside she felt like she'd shattered into a million pieces. Maria had even stolen their wave that they'd worked out *together*.

Maria returned, carrying a bag. "Shaylene and I are going shopping," she said to Kate. "Want to come?"

"No . . . uh . . . I can't. I've got . . . got some stuff to do," said Kate.

"Okay, see you later. Great about your part."

"Thanks," said Kate as she left for home. Neither Kate nor Maria gave a parting "camel wave."

• • •

Kate sat in her room in a state of shock. What had she done? How had she made Maria turn away from her? How could she make it better, how could she make it back to

115

how it was? If only she knew why Maria didn't want to be friends any more, it would be easier to take.

Kate flipped open her yearbook, to the picture of the two of them together at the Science Fair. It made Kate feel hot to read the verse below the picture, written in Maria's big, loopy handwriting. "Make new friends, but keep the old, one is silver but the other gold." Maria had drawn a heart around the word "gold," and there was the camel stamp in the corner. Kate wanted to tear the page out of the yearbook and throw it away, but there were other people's autographs on it, too. She looked at the red second–place ribbon on her bulletin board, and it seemed to mock her. Angrily, she tore it down, and tossed it under her bed. Maria's betrayal seemed to spoil the memory of the best time she'd had in all of Junior High. How dare Maria spoil Kate's memories! But when Kate thought about the future, she just felt awful and sick. How could she start high school without Maria there? Who would she talk about boys to? Who would she discuss the teachers and the homework and the dances with? She knew Maria would be in the in–crowd. Maria was pretty and popular, and always knew what to say. And when Kate was with Maria, she felt pretty and popular and like she knew what to say — though usually she didn't have to. What had she done to make Maria turn away? How could she make her turn back?

The ringing phone interrupted Kate's thoughts.

"Hi hon, I talked to Mr. Cormier, and everything is set."

Kate felt a little cheerier when she heard this news.

"In fact," her mom went on, "they'll have a tutor on set to help you keep up with your schoolwork, so things should work out fine."

"That's good." Kate didn't much want to think about schoolwork while it was still summer, but she knew this piece of news would go down well with her dad.

"Listen, hon, I've got to go to dinner with a client tonight, but dad will be home around six as usual."

"Oh . . . okay."

"There's some bolognese sauce left from last night if you like, or you guys can rustle up something else."

"No problem," said Kate. "See you later, then."

"Bye, honey!"

Just thinking about being on *Backbeat* again buoyed Kate's spirits a lot, but she was disappointed that her mom wouldn't be home because she had hoped to talk to her about Maria, and now she couldn't.

• • •

When Kate's dad came in, he seemed to be in a good mood. He poured himself his Scotch on the rocks and settled down in the living room with the newspaper. Kate looked up from reading the comics.

"So, did mom tell you she talked to Mr. Cormier?" she asked him.

"Yes, and she says there'll be a tutor on set. That's good news."

"I know," Kate replied.

"What say we order a pizza?" her dad suggested. "It saves us cooking and cleaning up."

"Okay," said Kate and went to the phone to place the order.

They sat in the kitchen with their pizza on paper towels. Kate stuffed a string of cheese from her chin into her mouth.

"I mean it about you keeping your marks up," Kate's dad commented. "This is high school now, and things are getting serious. Universities are starting to look at more than just your final year now, I understand."

Universities! All that seemed so remote to Kate. She still had high school to negotiate!

"Universities!" her dad was saying. "It seems so close. I don't feel old enough to have a daughter in high school yet!"

It didn't take them long to demolish the pizza. "I'm afraid I have a bit of work to do," he said. "Will you be all right by yourself down here?"

"Sure, Dad. I'm not a little kid." said Kate, though she wished he would stay.

As he went up the stairs, Kate tossed the pizza box and paper towels into the garbage and put the knife in the sink. Everything on TV was reruns that she didn't feel like watching again. Kate didn't feel like reading, and she was getting sick of Tetris. Finally, she decided to put on a CD. She began flipping though the disks and came upon the *Chorus Line* album. Kate hesitated, and then she decided to put it on. If Maria could steal their camel wave, Kate could keep Maria's half of the CD. If she couldn't dance with Maria, she'd dance by herself.

It felt awkward and hollow, doing "Hope I Get it" without Maria's counterpoint, and the cheery sound of "I Can Do That" didn't match Kate's mood. But then it was "At the Ballet," Kate and Maria's favourite, their pas de deux. It was so strange, waltzing alone, with her eyes closed. Suddenly, Kate heard her father's voice behind her.

"May I cut in?" he said, mock–formally.

Kate opened her eyes and looked at him in surprise.

"I remember when you were a little girl,

and you and I used to dance around this room," her dad went on. "Do you remember? You used to stand on my shoes."

"I remember," said Kate and raised her arms to dance with her dad. They began to waltz.

"I guess you don't need to stand on my shoes any more," said her dad, after a few moments. "You're half grown up, now."

"I know how to waltz now," laughed Kate.

"Don't you usually do this with Maria?" asked her dad.

"Maria . . . I guess she doesn't want to."

Dad stopped dancing for a moment and looked at her. "What do you mean?"

Kate kept on dancing, and he joined back in. "She's sort of not talking to me. I mean, she's talking to me, but it's not the same. She's just sort of — I don't know — thrown me aside."

"Why?" asked her dad, in surprise.

"I don't know." Kate buried her face in her dad's cotton shirt.

Her dad kept dancing. "Sometimes that happens," he said. "And there's no reason for it, and there's nothing you can do about it. People have reasons of their own, and Maria might not even know what hers are."

"But we were best friends," Kate protested. She wanted to wail. It hurt, it hurt.

"Things change. People change, even if

we wish they wouldn't." Just like what Kate's mom had said. "Maybe she wasn't true gold to begin with."

Funny her dad would say that, about gold. As the music reached its crescendo, Kate started to cry, and her dad stroked her hair.

Eleven

Five days later, Kate was at the Rolling
Films office, ready for the next read–through.
She was a little nervous going in, since the
regular cast members would all probably be
good buddies by now, and she didn't know
whether she would be able to fit in. She was
especially worried about Aimee, since they
really hadn't hit it off well. She still didn't get
along all that well with Tawny either.

Holly sent Kate into the big room she had
been in many times now, and John and
Natalie greeted her in a friendly way. At least
she got along with those two and Zack, who
now came puffing in.

"Omigosh . . . I'm not late . . . I can't
believe it," he sighed, plonking himself in a
chair, and fanning himself dramatically.

Mr. Cormier came in, unbuttoning his
suit jacket, and sat down at one end of the

table. Larry was next and Denise and Tawny, carrying an arm–load of scripts, came in chatting.

"Well, we're all here, I see," Mr. Cormier began, in his usual formal tones. "Firstly, you all know Kate. Please, let's welcome her to our regular cast as Julie."

The others applauded briefly, and Kate smiled. But inside, she felt wobbly all of a sudden. She thought she was just getting a recurring role. She didn't know she was official regular cast.

And where was Aimee?

As they read through their lines together, it became very clear that Aimee was gone. At first, Kate had no lines — the discussion was all about Diana having moved away, and what would they do without a bass player? But Julie was continuing to spy and eavesdrop. Besides that, she had a scene with no lines in which she bought a book on how to play bass, and later Julie was to sneak into the garage and fool around with the bass that was there. Eventually, though, she spoke, as she tried to become part of the band. Tawny's character — Sassy — was pretty disdainful of Julie, but reluctantly agreed to let her play for them. They accepted her into the band, but later Sassy decided that if Julie could play bass, *she* could play bass, and they didn't need Julie.

The climax of the story came when Sassy told Julie she was not wanted in the band. Julie countered with an emotional speech about not treating people like yo–yos, and the rest of the characters sided with Julie. Reluctantly, Sassy agreed to let Julie be part of the band.

At the end of the reading, everyone applauded and told Larry how terrific the script was. Denise told them all how terrific they were going to be — just as it had all gone last time, as if it was some part of the script not written down. Kate felt giddy. She couldn't believe she was sort of like the new Diana. She went home in a daze.

Kate had missed Tuesday's art class for wardrobe stuff, and although she could have got there just a little late today, she decided not to bother going. What was the point, really, since there were only a couple more classes, and she'd probably have to miss them for rehearsals or filming? Yet, even though she had not seen Maria for days, her so–called friend hadn't phoned or come over to find out where Kate had been.

Kate knew her mother was right — let it drag you down or rise above it — but it was hard, so hard to rise above it.

Rehearsals began Monday. Kate had all her lines memorized by Saturday. She played a lot of Tetris. Now she could even get scores of over 12,000 when she started at level ten. It was sort of driving her crazy — she felt addicted, yet she was bored. She really did have to get her mom to teach her to crochet.

Monday was the blocking rehearsal. Most of the others did not have all of their lines memorized, but Kate soon found that you didn't have to know them all, as you would for a play. You could just learn the ones for the scene, and then not worry about them too much, and learn the next scene. After a while, the correct lines just seemed like the only thing you *could* say in the situation.

Kate's big scene with the emotional speech, however, was a little different. For one thing, it was a long speech with no inter-ruptions. And for another, Kate was back to her old trouble, speaking too quickly.

"Thasnot fair. Iz not fair."

"Hang on, Kate," laughed Denise. "We've got a whole half hour to tell the story."

"Sorry," said Kate, starting again. "That's not fair. Snot fair." Kate stopped. "Sorry. It's not fair. I bought a book outa my own pere-root money" Slow down, Kate! "Even though I didn't know whether y'd take mere not. Oh, brother! Sorry."

"It's okay, Kate, you'll be fine," said Denise, who was fiddling, as usual, with her pendant. "Let's jump the speech. We'll work on it later. Let's move on to the next scene."

At the end of rehearsal, Denise called Kate over to one side.

"I know you're a little nervous at suddenly having a bigger part than you expected," Denise reassured her. "Don't worry, you'll get used to it, and you'll be fine. Remember, just breathe naturally, and say the words as though you really mean them, as though they're just coming to you as you say them. Just relax."

"Okay, Denise, I'll try. I'll be good . . . you'll see," Kate assured the director.

At home, Kate went over and over the big speech. She practised it a hundred times in the mirror. And gradually, just as it happened with the audition, it began to become a part of her, she began to make it hers.

• • •

Filming began a couple of days after the rehearsal. It had been over a week since she had seen or heard anything of Maria. It seemed amazing that Maria hadn't even called to see why she wasn't at art class — although Maria probably thought she was filming. Oh, well, she was just going to forget about it. But no way she was ever going to do a cow project or anything else with Maria again. It was funny how one day she was furious at her former friend, and the next day she was almost ready to forgive her — she just missed her so much!

The first days of filming included Kate's no–line scenes, and a couple of other straightforward scenes. But instead of feeling more confident by being in these simpler scenes, somehow Kate started feeling more nervous. She knew she could do her big speech by herself, in front of the mirror. But what about when all the other actors, all the crew — the Kirks, the Andys, the Colins, the Jens, the Pauls, the others, and Denise — were around. What if Mr. Cormier came on set that day, which Zack had told her he sometimes did? There were times, waiting in the green room, when Kate wished she had her Tetris game with her, so she could just watch the little squares fall and fall. But they weren't allowed to have computer games on set because the electronic noises they made drove everyone crazy.

Instead, Kate had taken to chewing wine gums. They took so long to chew through that they took care of most of her excess energy. And she liked their name — *wine gums*. They sounded sort of Englishy and classy.

She chomped through a red one while Natalie and she played their millionth game of checkers, waiting to be called on set. Sometimes there were others around, or Natalie was on set, but today it was just the two of them. As usual, Natalie won the game.

"Want to have another game?" Natalie asked.

"Nah," said Kate. "I'm tired of being beaten by a little kid."

Natalie was only a year younger than Kate, but she was so tiny that this had become a bit of a running joke on set.

"Have you started tap–dancing yet?" asked Kate.

"Yeah, want to see?"

"Sure," said Kate.

Natalie jumped up. "Okay, you know that song from *A Chorus Line*? The one at the end? That's what I'm dancing to." She started to sing. "One! La–la, La–la, La–lah! La–la, La–la, Lah, Lah, Lah."

Kate joined in, singing along with Natalie. Soon, Kate was singing, while Natalie talked through the steps. "Step, step, shuffle, ball–change, f–lap! ball–change," she recited. Soon the two of them were laughing, and Kate was showing Natalie the version she and Maria had choreographed.

• • •

The day came for Kate's scene. She wasn't needed in the morning, so it meant she didn't have to get up at six, as she did if she had an early call. She got up after her parents had

already left for work and had a leisurely
breakfast of peanut butter and bananas on
toast, with orange juice. She remembered
when she and Maria (Maria — the thought of
her made Kate wince) had gone to the training that first day, and she couldn't even swal-
low breakfast. Afterwards, she strolled down
to the corner to stock up on wine gums.

She pulled open the door, and the bell
jangled as she stepped in. There, in the tiny
store, she found herself face to face with
Maria.

TWELVE

Kate breathed in sharply. Although she hadn't been thinking about it, deep down she had known this moment would have to come sometime. And because she hadn't been thinking about it, she had no idea how to react.

Maria spoke first. "Oh . . . hi, Kate!" she said, full of friendliness. "Long time no see!"

"That's right," said Kate tightly.

"So, what've you been doing with yourself? You weren't at art class."

"No, I've been filming," replied Kate. Why was Maria being so nice?

"Well, see ya," said Maria, and she started past Kate. "Have fun filming. Don't be a stranger."

Kate was left gaping, and Maria was almost out the door, when she found her voice. "Maria!" she called after her.

Maria turned, and Kate walked a couple of steps toward her, away from the shopkeeper.

"Don't do that," Kate said, in a low voice.

"Do what?" asked a startled Maria.

"Mess around with me like that. Don't do it. Don't 'forget' to call me to go to the movies, don't make jokes about me behind my back and then act all nicey–nice with me when you're not with your other friends. I'm not your yo–yo to play with. Don't pretend we're friends when you couldn't even care less what I've been doing, where I am, or how I feel. I *am* a stranger."

"What are you talking about? I can have other friends. We're not married."

" 'Make new friends, Maria, but keep the old.' Remember? But I'm not sure you *are* gold."

"You are so . . . you are so . . . you get so stuck on things. You're such a stick–in–the mud."

"No, Maria. I'm loyal. But not to people who show they're not worth it."

Maria stood there speechless, unmoving. Kate returned her stare for an instant, then jangled out of the corner store and walked away. It was only when she was halfway down the block that she realized that she'd forgotten to buy wine gums. But she didn't care. Adrenalin was pumping through her — she felt strong.

• • •

Later, as Kate sat on the bus on the way to the studio, the reality started to hit her. What she had just said meant that she and Maria could probably never be friends again. Oh, great! Just what she needed on the very day she should have been at her best for filming. And instead, she felt sad and angry and hurt and used. She felt more like crying than acting. But she couldn't cry, she had work to do. Besides, crying would give her red eyes.

When she arrived, Kate let Holly know she was there, and then went straight to the dressing room she now shared with Natalie and Tawny. It wasn't quite Hollywood glitz. They did have a big mirror with lights around it, like the ones you see in the movies, with a table in front of it and three chairs. A coat–rack on one side held their clothing for the episode. Pamela had Kate in slightly more interesting clothes for this episode than the shorts and T–shirts of the paper girl part — a flowered vest had been added as well as a few large beads on a leather thong around her neck, and the shorts were a more fashionable style. The three girls now had a bank of three lockers for them to put their stuff in. And that was it. Kate suspected it was left plain so they would go into the green room and mix with the others, but right now she didn't feel like talking to anyone. Luckily, neither Natalie nor Tawny was around right now — especially Tawny. Kate didn't have as much trouble with Tawny as with Aimee, but she wasn't her favourite person.

Kate thought about Aimee a little — it had been Zack who had told her what had happened to her. Pretending to be a Hollywood star, Zack had struck a pose, fluffed an imaginary bouffant hairstyle, pursed his lips, and said in a silky voice, "I'm ready for my close–up now, Mr. DeMille."

It was particularly funny, because Zack himself looked more like Barney Rubble than Marilyn Monroe, yet he did have the essence of Aimee's flirtatious show–offiness in his impersonation. Apparently Aimee's attitude and bad manners rubbed everyone the wrong way, and Mr. Cormier gave her the boot. It had made everyone on set really cautious in episode two, and Kate would have loved to have known what Tawny thought of it all. But by now, episode three, everybody was back to normal. It made Kate nervous, though, because if Aimee could be fired, so could she. Even the way the script was, Julie could disappear after the next episode. They could write in the next one that Sassy gets her way and gets rid of Julie. She had to be good today, and she was a mess.

It wasn't long before she was called on set. This was it, the big scene. She felt tingly and kind of like she was walking on a

133

waterbed, sort of like the ground wasn't quite behaving like it was supposed to. Denise called for a run–through while the crew made some small adjustments to the lighting.

"Just go through the lines — don't worry about performance right now," Denise told them.

The scene started with a short conversation among the four original band members, and then Kate's Julie arrived. Kate was to go over, pick up the bass, and then Sassy would tell her there'd been a change of plans, and Julie wasn't in the band any more. Julie was to ask why, and Sassy's answer was that if Julie could teach herself to play bass, then so could Sassy, so they didn't need her. That was when Kate's big speech came.

Kate walked through her speech — she knew she had a good delivery of it when she was "on," but she didn't want to use up what little emotional energy she had on this peculiar day.

"Good, Kate," said Denise. "And I know you'll speak a little more slowly and clearly when we film."

The master shot was done for the first part of the scene, and Denise then asked for a new set–up, to do Kate's big speech in close–up. The actors took a short break while the crew set up the new shot. Denise took Kate aside to talk to her about the scene.

"Now, don't be nervous," she told Kate. "You don't have to get it all in one take. We're going to be shooting the reactions of the other cast members after this, and they'll be pieced into your speech in editing. So if you mess up a line or a word, just go back and pick up the sentence from the beginning — we can cut out the mistakes. And if you get all lost, we can stop and start over. It's okay, and I don't want you to worry."

Kate nodded. Somehow, instead of taking the pressure off, this was making her feel even more nervous. The fact that Denise had taken her aside made her feel like it was a Big Deal. And in spite of Denise's assurances, she knew film stock was expensive, and every foot they shot cost money. As she worried, she realized that she had begun fiddling with the beads at her neck. She noticed again that Denise didn't tug at her pendant when she was actually directing. It was like there was a law that *somebody* had to be yanking at jewellery, so if Denise didn't, someone else did.

In no time, they were ready for filming. Kate adjusted her vest, shook her curls, and tried to throw away all her Kate thoughts: Maria, the cost of the film, Aimee being fired, the fact that there was even a camera there. She tried to step into Julie and ignore everything else. As she moved mentally into her role, she had an idea.

"Ready?" called Denise.

"Rolling!" confirmed Colin.

"And speed," said Andy — which meant his recording equipment was going smoothly.

Kirk jumped in with the clapper board, just like the kind they have in Hollywood movies. "Scene twenty–one, shot two, take one!" he said, and snapped the top clapper shut just before jumping out of camera range.

"And ... action," said Denise, cueing Tawny by pointing at her. They were setting up Julie's speech by having Kate come off Sassy's previous line.

" ... so we don't need you, you see," she said.

Kate waited two beats, blinked once and clacked her beads. Finally, she said, quietly, "That's not fair. It's not fair. I worked hard to learn to play this instrument. I bought a book out a m'own paperoute money ... " Kate realized she was speeding up and paused before going on. "Even though I didn't know whether you'd take me or not. I d'serve t'be in this band." Out of the corner of her eye, she realized she could see Zack, who was off–camera, with his hands at his temples, subtly wiggling his fingers. It was Kate and Maria's old signal, the dying bug, bleeding blue–black blood. Suddenly, out of nowhere, all her feelings about Maria came rushing up — all her nerves, her emotion, her anger, her hurt at being treated like a yo–yo by her supposed best friend, came rushing up, like a flame. "I deserve to be in this band," Kate went on, speaking slowly, emotionally, fire and ice in her voice. Gradually, her hand came away from the necklace. "I earned my way into this band, and you can't kick me out. I'm part of it now and I have a say. You can't treat me like some kind of yo–yo, toss me away, yank me back, toss me away." Kate stopped, stared defiantly at Tawny, who stared defiantly back. Everyone held their breath for a moment, until Denise shouted, "Cut! All *right*! Got it in one! Nice touch with the beads, Kate."

Suddenly, cast and crew began to applaud, and Kate didn't know what to do. She felt wobbly, then suddenly exhausted. Zack gave her a conspiratorial grin, and even Tawny looked impressed. But Kate could hardly feel a thing. She plonked herself down on a stool in the garage and said in a small voice, "Could I have a glass of juice, please?"

A taste of what's to come in

BACKBEAT

A square of white paper appeared on the table. John glanced up, to face a smiling, giggling, wriggling girl. Behind her were two more.

"Can you put, 'To Erin'?" the girl asked, " . . . and put something else, you know, something *neat*."

Oh no. Another one who thought that John was really Bryce, the smooth–talking lead guitar player from *Backbeat*. John felt his mouth go dry.

"To Erin," he wrote, and hesitated. What could he write that this girl would think was neat? He wished Zack were here — or Kate. They always knew what to do. "Keep watching *Backbeat*. John Pappas," he scrawled on the paper.

The girl giggled. "Say something," she ordered him.

John felt his throat close. He looked at her, and gave her a lopsided grin — it usually worked.

A trio of little shrieks erupted, and the girls stepped back.

"Ohmigod!" squealed one.

"He's so *cute!*" came the second.

The one called Erin bit her fist.

John breathed a little easier — for the moment — and wondered where he could get a face transplant.

Look for the next *Backbeat* story — coming soon.